# BALOR'S REVENGE

A
novel by
Paul Fronda

Balor's Revenge

First published in the United Kingdom in 2016
by Paul Fronda

Cover design by Martin Smith

Edited by Sheila Fronda

Proofread by Sheila Fronda

ISBN 978-0-9930132-9-4

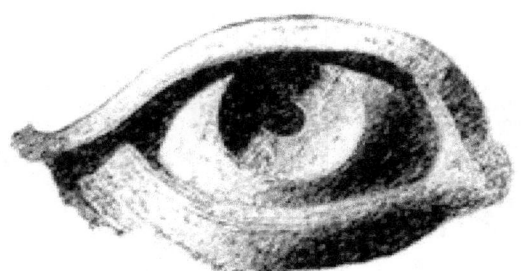

# Forward

The quietness of the room was broken by the creak of the door opening and closing.

"Evening, Danny.  Why all the hush?"

"Evening, Michael.  Old Duffy is spinning one of his yarns to the Americans," Danny said, producing a pint of Michael's usual.

"Not the leprechaun tales again?"

"No, we haven't heard this one before."

"Sh...sh," came from several others in the pub as all ears were listening to Duffy's tale.

"Have I missed much?" Michael whispered.

"No, he's only just begun," Danny whispered back. "He's just explained that the story starts with a couple in New York."

# Chapter 1

"Sean, Honey, there's mail here for you," Becky called upstairs to her husband.

"I'm not expecting any; who's it from?" he called down from the bathroom.

"How do I know? It's addressed to you; but it has an Irish stamp on it. It's on the table. I'll be in the laundry room."

Sean came noisily downstairs. He picked up the mail and studied the envelope. On the back was: Kieran & Donegan Solicitors, Cork. He pulled out a chair and sat down, staring at the envelope.

"Are you going to open it or just stare at it all day?" Becky said, coming into the room.

"I wonder what it's about. I don't know anyone in Ireland."

"And you're not going to know, unless you open it," Becky said drily.

Sean sliced the envelope open with a knife, took out the letter and read it.

"Well, what does it say?" Becky said, mildly curious.

"It says that my grandfather has passed away and that I have inherited his estate," he announced in surprise.

"I didn't know you had a grandfather, especially in Ireland," Becky said.

"Nor did I. Well, not alive. Dad never talked much about his father when I was a child and then when we left I didn't think anymore about my Irish roots.

"Was he rich?"

"As I said, I don't know anything about him. It says that, if I could come to Cork, they would be able to tell me more about the estate."

"It sounds as if he was rich - mentioning an *estate.* Maybe it's a farm, or acres of land. Does it say whereabouts in Ireland?"

"Slow down, Becky. It probably means I've inherited a goat, or a donkey or something small like that. Remember, this is Ireland we're talking about."

"Surely they wouldn't want you to travel all that way, just to reveal you've inherited a goat? They could have said that in a letter."

"Probably."

"So when do we leave?"

"Do you know how far it is from New York to Ireland, Becky?"

"Not really."

"About 3,000 miles. That's about a seven-hour flight to Dublin, and then who knows how far it is from there to Cork?"

"Can't we fly straight to Cork, to save time?"

"Not as far as I know. It has to be Dublin, but we could take a flight from Dublin to Cork. If we do go, it would be nicer by car, and a great way to see Southern Ireland."

"Are you saying we're going then?"
"I said *if,* Becky.  And where are you going now?
"To pack."


Becky looked down at the patchwork of green below.
"So that's the Emerald Isle?"
"Yes, King Oisin O'Reilly's kingdom."
"Who?"
"King Oisin O'Reilly, King of the Leprechauns."
"And I thought you were Sean," she laughed.
"I wouldn't laugh too much.  Ireland's a land of folklore and mystery that goes back hundreds of years.  My Dad used to tell me stories of the leprechauns and their pot of gold, every night before I went to sleep."
"I suppose the minute we get there, you'll be out looking for that gold then?" she laughed.
"You'll keep."


\*       \*       \*       \*       \*


"There you are, Danny!  I *knew* he couldn't resist bringing leprechauns into the story!  I tell you, there'll be more later - as sure as my name's Michael," he said, leaning back on
his bar stool.
Old Duffy stopped talking and gave Michael a look.
"Sorry, Duffy," Michael said quietly.
Duffy continued with his story.

"It looks so green from up here."

"That's why it's called the Emerald Isle."

"Yes, I knew that. I was just saying."

"You know, Beck, looking down on it, it's as if something inside is telling me I'm home."

"That's the Irish blood in you. You did tell me once about how your father came to the States but I've forgotten; remind me."

"I don't know how many greats, but great-grandfather, Finbar Finñegan was a tenant farmer. He was forced to move to England when the great potato famine took hold."

"Oh, when was that?"

"I can tell you exactly when it was," he said turning over a book on his lap. I brought this 'History of Ireland" with me so we could find out more about just that kind of thing."

"I wondered what that was. It is from your collection?"

"Yes, Dad used to read it to me when I was little," he said flicking through the pages. "Here we are:

'As a direct consequence of the famine, Ireland's population of almost 8.4 million in 1844 had fallen to 6.6 million by 1851. The majority lost were labourers and smallholders, so land ownership became concentrated into fewer hands.' Do you know about one million people died from starvation, or from typhus and other famine-related diseases?"

"That's awful."

"The number of Irish who emigrated during the famine may have reached two million. By the time

Ire and achieved independence in 1921, its population was barely half of what it had been in the early 1840s."

"So what happened to Finbar? Did he ever go back?"

"Yes, with his son, Shamus, after making his fortune and marrying an English girl."

"So I take it your grandad was rich, hence the letter from the solicitors."

"Who knows, Becks. That was a long time ago, and anything could have happened. As I said, it's probably a goat."

"So, your father grew up in Ireland?"

"Yes, but he fell out with *his* father over business. (I was just a young lad at the time.) Because my dad knew how close my grandad was to me, he decided the most hurtful way he could get even with him was to put some distance between us by moving to America, where I met you, Becks."

Becky put her head on his shoulder.

"You've never spoken much about your father, and I've never asked. I knew you would have talked about him if you wanted to. Is he still alive?"

"I don't know. One day he was there, then he wasn't. Mum tried to find him and heard that he'd talked about going to make amends with his father. She thought it was just talk after too many drinks. Soon the months passed, then the years and, as we didn't hear from him, we forgot him."

"Why didn't your mother track him down, knowing where he might have gone? Didn't she love him?"

"Would you love me if I had come home drunk every night? No, it was a merciful release for her."

"Well, I think your mother brought you up well. To think, if she had taken you back to Ireland to find him, I would never have met you."

"You see - there's always something good that comes out of adversity."

"Just one thing: I guess, as your grandad left everything to you, your father never did patch things up between them?"

"I like to think they did, but it sounds unlikely doesn't it? The seat belt light is on, Becky. It won't be long now."

"Exciting!" she replied, squeezing his hand.

In a short while the plane had landed.

"Now are you sure you want to get going, or do you want to check in at a hotel and be refreshed for tomorrow?" he asked.

"As it's only a couple of hours' drive, let's get going. Unless you're too tired?"

"I am a bit, but I'm sure a couple of hours won't hurt before I get my head down."

Having signed for the hire car, they were soon on their way towards Cork.

"Don't forget you have to drive on the left," she reminded him.

"I know what side. I'm trying to listen to the sat-nav to get us on the right road."

"Sorry, Honey."

"We've got all day, so let's take the scenic route. It's slower and a bit further, but as I said before, if we're going to do it, we might as well see the real Ireland at its best - especially Waterford."

"Are you sure you're not too tired?"

"I'll be okay and, if I find I'm getting tired, I can always pull over for five minutes."

"Well, as long as you do. Isn't it Waterford that's known for its crystal glass?" she asked enthusiastically.

"That's the place."

"Look Sean! There's one of those Irish horse wagons," she said as they drove past. "Can we go back and take a photo?"

"It's a tinker's caravan. Did you know there are around ten thousand tinkers in the United States?"

"I knew there were some, but not that many," she replied.

"Apparently, they were descendants of travellers who left Ireland, mostly during the period between 1845 and 1860 during the Great Famine. Did you know that there are about 2,500 of them living in Murphy Village, a community outside North Augusta, South Carolina?"

"No, I didn't. It appears they went everywhere back then. So, can we go back? You said there's no hurry, and surely Ireland doesn't come better than that?"

"Okay, but don't buy anything."

"I only want a photo."

"The old lady there will sell you the horse if she has her way."

"Hi there. Can my wife take a photo?"

"Is that all you want?" she said, looking at them shrewdly.

"We're not here to buy anything, just a photo."

"Sean, don't be rude."

"You have to make it clear with tinkers," he replied quietly.

"Sorry about that," Becky said.

"You can have a photo, but first you must let me do something for you," the old tinker said.

"And what is that?" Sean asked cautiously.

"To give you a word."

"What sort of word would that be?" Sean said in a flippant voice.

"First you have to give, in order to receive; it's the order that's laid down."

"I knew it! You can't even take a photo without it costing."

"Sean! How much?" Becky said, searching in her bag for some money. Becky knew all about the principles of giving and receiving from church.

"Anything, as long as it is a coin," the old lady replied.

Becky produced a dollar and gave it to her. The old lady took it without looking at it and put it in her pocket.

"Come with me, Cailin," she said, leading Becky up the wooden steps to the caravan.

Becky stood at the top of the steps, turned and said to Sean, "You going to be okay while I go in?"

"Sure. You go and have fun. I'll go and talk to the old horse" he chuckled.

The inside was colourfully decorated. The old lady sat down behind a small table and gestured with her hand for Becky to take a seat opposite.

"Give me your hand," she said.

Becky played along with her request and laid her hand palm up on the table.

"Cailin, you seen too many films. I don't work like that," the old lady said, holding her hand tightly.

She looked into Becky's eyes and said nothing. A minute passed, then she said, "Your roots are not here. It's the strong call of Irish roots which draw your husband's family line home." She paused for a short while and then, with concern in her voice, she said, "Take heed, Cailin. Go back now with your husband and child while you can! For what lies ahead is an ill wind that waits for you. It is not the will of God that such fate awaits, but take heed of him that waits for you."

"Who's he?" Becky asked.

"It is a name that's so evil that I will not let it from my lips. Four more warnings are given and four chances of going back have been set. You would be foolish not to accept them. Concern yourselves with the number eight. It is assigned to your husband, and it is a number that will seal his fate in stone if you choose to stay. But the boy you carry must be protected from *him*, as he seeks to destroy him. May the good saints protect you and bless you today, and may troubles ignore you each step of the way."

The old lady let go of her hand. The smile that Becky went in with had disappeared from her face.

"That's all Cailin," she said, standing up. "Take this and put it around the child's neck; may God protect you all." As she spoke, the old woman placed a coin with a strange cross shape on it into Becky's hand.

As she made her way down the wooden steps, Sean was about to make a joke, but the look on his wife's face made him ask: "Everything all right, Becks?"

"Can we go?" she said, walking back to the car.

The old lady called after them, "Don't look into his eye! Protect the boy!"

"What did she say, Becks? You look worried."

"Can we just drive?"


A few miles up the road he asked her, "So, what did she say to make you look so worried?"

Becky told him.

"I'm not having her scare you like that with a load of old rubbish! We're going back!"

"Please, I'm alright."

But Sean wasn't having it. He swung the car around and headed back.

"I'm sure it wasn't this far back. I know we'd only travelled a couple of miles.

"Maybe it is a bit further, Sean."

"Okay, I'll drive on a bit more, but I really don't think it's this far."

Eventually he stopped the car.

"No, it's definitely not this far. We'll go back. Somehow we've gone past her."

"There's the spot! I recognise that white field gate where the caravan was." Becky said, pointing.

Pulling in, he said, "But that's impossible. A horse-drawn caravan couldn't have moved that fast - with that old horse, and there weren't any turnings, Beck."

"Well, you did say Ireland was a land of mystery," she said with a wry smile.

"Yeah, I did say that, didn't I? Anyway, the smile's back on your face; that's all that matters. Shall we go?"

"The old lady kept calling me 'Cailin'. Do you think she thought that was my name?"

"No, it's Irish for 'girl'."

"Well... she was right there, wasn't she?"

"Of course, Becks."

"Blow! With all that distraction, I forgot to take a photo," Becky said.

"While you were in the van being told a lot of old blarney, I took one on my phone."

"Great. Can I see?"

Sean handed her the phone.

"There's nothing there, it didn't take."

"Of course it's there! Scroll down."

"Nope. No photo at all," she replied.

"That's a shame. I don't know why."


"You look deep in thought, Becks"

"Sorry, Honey, I was just looking at what the old lady gave me. It brought back her words."

"What is it?"

"It's a coin with a cross on it. It looks very old." Turning it over, she said, "Oh, I didn't see what was on the other side. There's an inscription. Is that Irish?"

Sean, who was driving, glanced at it and said, "I'm not sure, but it looks Gaelic. Listen, it's probably a bit of cheap tat. It's all part of a big act put on for us tourists, and we walked right into it."

"Probably. But she sounded so convincing, with the warning. What do you think she meant about four warnings and chances. Oh, and the number eight? But most of all it was those words: 'Don't look into his

eye' that disturbed me, Sean. Whose eye do you think she meant?"

"It means nothing. As I said, it's all an act. She said that to add a bit of drama and mystery to it."

"She also told me to go back home with you and *the child*, and something about protecting the child."

"Well, that proves it's an act. We don't have a child do we?"

"No."

"Well, there you are then."


"You're not pregnant are you?"

"No! Well, I don't think so . . ."

They both looked at each other.

# Chapter 2

"Where exactly are we now, Honey?"

"We're coming into Thomastown. Next stop is Waterford, where we can get a bite to eat and a look round the factory. Is that okay?"

"Yep. Maybe we can buy something nice to take home with us."

"I'm sure we will."


After they'd eaten, Sean asked Becky if she was too tired for the factory.

"No, I'm fine. We'll catch up with sleep in Cork."

"Hey, Becks, we're just in time. They're just about to start a guided tour."

The tour guide started to speak to the people around him.

"Just a few words to explain what you will see this afternoon. We will learn about the history of Waterford Crystal from its earliest days; watch skilled artisans

blow, cut, sculpt and engrave crystal; and explore the retail shop's shining and elegant wares."

"Can't wait for the shop bit, Honey."

"Well did you enjoy that, Becks?" Sean said, getting into the car.

"It was great. I've just got to get it back home in one piece. I must confess I'm looking forward to that bed. How long before Cork?"

"Give me a second, sat-nav is saying: Kilmacthomas, Dungarvan, Youghal, Midleton, Cork. 1.55 minutes, 62 miles."

"That long!"

"Well, I did say this route would be longer. If we'd used the motorway, we would have been there by now - but then you wouldn't have experienced the old tinker entertainment or bought your glassware."

"No, I'm not complaining. You know what I'm like when I'm tired."

"Why don't you close your eyes, and I'll wake you when we're there."

"Wake me if you see anything interesting."

"I will."

"Promise?"

"I promise."

As the miles passed, Sean was experiencing a feeling of contentment, being in Ireland. Every now and then he reached over to gently lift Becky's head off her chest and back onto the seat. A little smile came across his face as her nose twitched from a fly that had got into the car. He could see the light was

fading and was hoping they could make Cork before nightfall, as the roads were narrow and winding in some places. Also he had noticed that they hadn't passed anyone on the road, not even a tractor - which was unusual, even for this part of Ireland. As much as he tried, he couldn't get the thought out of his head that the road wouldn't be a good place to be if the car should break down.

He had turned off the sat-nav so it wouldn't wake Becky but he was quite confident of the route as he had memorised the places he had to go through. By his reckoning, they should have passed through Dungarvan by now but, glancing at his watch, he could see that they had been travelling for over an hour. He knew that somehow he must have gone wrong. He turned the sat-nav back on, hoping to find out where he was, but to his dismay the screen was blank. For some reason it wasn't working.

The darkness had now taken hold. His concerns were multiplying and he could feel the 'what-ifs' trying to take control. He wondered if he should wake Becky, but then if he did she would only worry.

"Oh no, that's all I need - fog!" he said out loud.

Becky stirred and said in a sleepy voice, "Did you say something, Honey?"

"No, Becky, go back to sleep."

She made a little murmur and closed her eyes.

Sean reduced his speed to a crawl, trying to negotiate the road. With the wipers on, he could just make out that there was a narrow, humpback bridge a little way ahead. As he got closer he could see a figure pointing, apparently directing him to go back the way he had just come.

For the last half hour Sean had been desperate to find someone to ask where he was, yet the shock of this unexpected appearance made him hit the brakes. The sudden stop made Becky shoot forward, taking up the slack of her seat belt. Sean turned to see if she was all right, concerned that the jolt may have woken her. Amazed that it hadn't, he fumbled for the switch to lower his window and ask the man for directions. But there was no one there.

Sean sat there, trying to figure out whether what he had just seen was real or the result of jet lag and desperately *wanting* to see someone. He knew that, whatever it was, sitting there wasn't going to get them to Cork.

The experience at the bridge was now some miles behind him. He glanced over to see that Becky was still asleep. As quietly as he could, he started to tap on the sat-nav screen but it was futile. The only direction he could take was onwards, hoping it might take them to Cork.

As much as he didn't want Becky to worry, he wished she was awake as he could do with her companionship. The feeling of being alone in the dark lanes made him feel uneasy. The only consolation was that the fog had lifted, but then the wind had picked up and it had started to rain hard. The wipers were only just coping with it and Sean found himself sitting on the edge of the seat, struggling to see as the headlight glare was reflecting on the wet surface.

"This is a nightmare," he said to himself. The last time he had experienced conditions like this was

when he and Becky had gone camping. It had been a spur of the moment decision, to surprise Becky one weekend. She taught language skills and had been finding it stressful, saying that she longed for a break.

"Pack a weekend bag. I'm taking you away," he had said to her.

"Where are we going? Five star hotel?' she had asked, excited at the thought of luxury.

"Could be," he'd said vaguely, as he'd wanted it to be a big surprise. She had never been camping before and it would be something different, to take her mind off the campus.

The look on her face when they'd pulled up in the woods had made him chuckle. He could hear her now, "What we doing here?"

"Camping."

He could still hear her saying, *Camping*?" as it echoed through the woods.

"It will be fun, Becks; something we've never done before. It'll take your mind off work; you'll be able to relax. We're miles away from anyone, alone with nature."

"Good. Then no one will see me kill you!" she had said, angry and disappointed.

"Well, it's almost five star. I hired a good tent," he had said, producing it from the trunk of the car.

"Almost five star! You could fit my sister's miniature poodle in that!"

"Come on, Becks. Where's your sense of adventure? Give me a hand to put it up. It'll be cosy . . ."

"Well, at least it's a nice day and it won't be cold," she had said, softening towards the idea.

"That's the spirit, Becks."

A mighty crack of thunder in the middle of the night had woken them. It had been followed by gale-force winds and rain, so heavy that the floor of the tent had had a stream of water running through it. Becky had got up and said, "If you want to camp, you can stay here. I'm sleeping in the car!"

With that she'd scurried to the car and locked the doors, leaving Sean banging on the window and shouting, "Becks, open the door! Let me in - I'm getting drenched!"

"What are you chuckling about, Honey?"

"Oh, you're awake! I was miles away."

"How long has it been raining? Where are we?"

"It's been raining some time, Becks. It reminded me of the time I took you camping.

"Yeah, well it wasn't anything to laugh about."

"Maybe not at the time, but you must admit, Becks, looking back you can see the funny side?"

"Shall we say camping is not on my list of things to do ever again?"

"But you do forgive me don't you?" he said turning towards her.

"Sean . . . !"

Standing in the middle of the lane, facing them, was a young girl, pointing to the way they had just come. It was too late to avoid hitting her. The tyres screeched loudly on the wet road, causing the car to skid off the lane, missing the trees but burying the front in the hedgerow.

"You okay?" he said, turning to Becky. "Stay here."

Unfastening his seatbelt, he rushed out of the car, fearing the worst. He was expecting to see the child lying on the road, but there was nothing. He checked the ditch and hedgerow, but still there was no sign of her. He walked back to the car.

"Sean, please tell me we didn't hit her."

"The thing is, Becky, I can't find her."

"What do mean, you can't find her? Have you checked the sides of the lane?"

"Yes. I'm telling you, there's nothing there."

'I saw her standing there. There's no way we didn't hit her, Sean."

"I know. I only saw her for a split second, but she was there all right."

"What was a young child doing in the middle of the lane? It was all so quick, but I'm sure she was pointing at us - as if she was trying to tell us something."

"Like what?"

"Don't know. What do we do now? We can't just drive off, can we?"

"We'll have to get the car back onto the lane before we do."

"Where are we anyway, Sean?"

"Let's sort the car out first."

The more he revved, the more the tyres sunk into the mud.

"I'm going to have to get out and push. Can you sit behind the wheel and rev?"

The wind and rain seemed to increase as he tried with all his might to push, but the car just sunk deeper and deeper.

"Move over, Becks. It's no use," he said getting back into the car, soaking wet.

"What are we going to do, Sean?"

"We call for help," he said, getting his phone out. However, there was no signal.

"We have a choice. Either I go and try to find help, or we stay here till morning and hopefully someone will come along."

"I don't like the idea of being on my own, not knowing how long you'll be gone. And I don't relish sleeping here, but what choice do we have?"

"We don't, Becks, but try your phone just in case."

"No signal."

"That settles it. We sleep in the car."

"So, where are we?"

"Somewhere between Kilmactomas and Dungarvan."

"What do you mean *somewhere*? Won't the sat-nav tell you?"

"It's not working. I've been trying to get it going, but it's completely dead."

"I don't understand. It's been nearly three hours since we left Waterford and you said it was two hours to Cork, but we haven't even reached Dung . . . something."

"Dungarvan."

"Whatever! So what's gone wrong, Sean?"

"I switched the sat-nav off so it wouldn't wake you. I was doing all right; I knew what the next place was and with a direct route I couldn't go wrong, but then it came over foggy and I got lost. I just don't know how, Becks, honestly."

"Well, if we're here for the night I'll need my coat from the trunk."

Already soaked, Sean quickly got out and brought back her coat.

Becky covered herself with it and tried to get to sleep, but the noise of the wind and rain outside made it almost impossible. She was only able to drift in and out. As Sean hadn't slept for some time, it didn't take him long to doze off.

Becky was woken from her light sleep. The wind and rain had stopped, but she could hear the sound of distant, enchanted music. She strained to hear where it was coming from.        "Sean," she whispered, "are you awake?"    There was no response, and she realised he was in a deep sleep.

She looked at her watch. It was 12 o'clock. She knew what she was about to do was crazy, venturing outside on her own in the night, but the light of a full moon seemed to take away the scariness. It was as f the music had enchanted her and was calling her to it. Unable to resist, she opened the door quietly and made her way to where she thought it was coming from. The thick hedgerow was stopping her, so she followed it along and found an opening, which led her into a wood. Quietly she went from tree to tree as she could hear the music getting nearer. Then, from behind a tree, she could see in a clearing, a sight that could only be from a fantasy tale.

Sitting on tree stumps were two little people, one was playing a flute and the other the fiddle. In the middle of the circle was a third, dancing to the music. His coat was red and he had ginger hair and beard, whereas the others had green coats with white hair and beards. The word 'leprechauns' came to mind. She had always joked with Sean when he tried to convince her they were real, and she knew he was

just teasing her.  If she told him about this, he would never believe her!  *Photo.  Yes!  It would be proof!*

She took out her phone and selected 'camera'. Moving quietly, she stepped out from behind the tree, aimed the camera and clicked.  The flash lit up the area and, in the blink of the eye, the little people had scattered.  Becky walked over to where they had been and noticed, on the ground where the one in red had been dancing, a tiny knurled stick. She bent down and picked it up to get a closer look.  From behind a bush, she heard whisped chatter.  She knew they were hiding.

"I won't hurt you!  I didn't mean to scare you. Please, show yourselves again," Becky  called softly. The chattering stopped, then she heard movement.

The little one in the red coat stepped out and said, "If you give me my knock, I will grant you your desire," he said, holding out his hand.

"Knock?  What's that?"  she replied.

"My *shillelagh*!  You have in your hand!" he said crossly.

"Sorry, I didn't mean to pick it up," she said bending down to give it to him.

"Thank you.  For that I will grant you your desire, but first let me introduce myself: Oisin O'Reilly, King of the Leprechauns," he said, bowing down with his hat in his hand.

The thought came to her mind: *Sean was right then.  They are real.*

"Of course we're real!  We're as real as you," he said, even more cross.

"How did you know what I was thinking?"

"I'm King of the Leprechauns. It's my job to know everything. If I didn't, my name wouldn't be Oisin O'Reilly."

"How do you do, King of the Leprechauns. My name's Becky," she said playing along, as she began to suspect this wasn't real. "I'll have to get back to my husband; he will be wondering where I've got to," she said, stifling a laugh. "Can I ask you something, King?"

"Is this your desire you are asking for?"

"No . . . "

"Because I'll only grant you one!" he said impatiently.

"Why were you dancing?"

"It's my job, as it was the king's before and from the beginning of time, that we dance the new day in. Why, was my dancing not good?"

"Yes, it was a good dance; the best I have ever seen from a leprechaun."

"That would be a *King* of the Leprechauns," he replied abruptly.

"Yes, of course. That's what I meant - King." *What am I doing, having a conversation with a fairytale?* "I'll have to go," she announced.

"You cannot go until you have your desire. You see, once a human has seen me it is written in our law that I must grant them their desire. Now what will it be?"

Becky thought for a moment. Because she had decided this wasn't real, she didn't bother asking for anything big. The little king standing there, waiting patiently and leaning on his shillelagh, said, "So what will it be?"

"Well, my desire is that our car, which is stuck in the hedge, will be freed."

"Granted!" he said, banging the shillelagh to the ground.

\*     \*     \*     \*     \*

Leaning on the bar, Michael spoke out loudly, "I *said* he would Danny! Didn't I tell you? He just can't resist a story of the leprechauns."

"Well, at least it's a different one this time, Michael."

Duffy looked over at them and winked.

"He sure knows how to give the Americans a good tale."

"To be sure, Michael, that he does!" Danny replied.

\*     \*     \*     \*     \*

The sudden knocking on Sean's window startled them awake.

"You two okay in there?" It was the voice of a ginger-bearded man.

Sean quickly got out of the car. "At last! I thought we would never see anyone. We skidded off the lane last night."

"I can see that, to be sure; it looks like you'll be needing a little help to get it back on the road. Gilroy O'Malley - at your service."

"If you can, Gilroy, that would be great," Sean replied, relieved.

"I'll just unhitch the trailer from old Molly, and we'll have you out of there. Your little missy might be wanting to get out before we do."

Having unhitched the trailer from his tractor, Gilroy backed it up to the car and connected a chain. Within seconds the car was back on the lane.

"Apart from a few scratches, I cannot see any damage," Gilroy said, cheerfully.

"Thanks! I don't know what we'd have done if you hadn't come along," Sean replied.

"You must have had the Irish luck rub off on you. Nobody uses this lane anymore, since the new road was built. The only reason *I'm* here is that I decided to move a few sheep from my farm to a field up the lane today. Normally I wouldn't have moved them for a couple of weeks, but I woke up this morning and said to Molly (that's my wife, not my tractor. I named the tractor after her because it's been an old faithful thing, never letting me down). Where was I?"

"You were saying that you wouldn't normally have moved your sheep," Sean reminded him.

"Ah yes! As I was saying, to be sure - you were lucky. It would have been a long time before anyone found you, if you'd just sat there. But how did you get on this lane? It's been closed for years. Which way did you come?"

"I don't know. We had just come through Kilmacthomas and followed what I thought was the road to Dungarvan; then it came over foggy and then the storm and we ended up here. I only saw one person on the lane, just before an old stone bridge but

he seemed to walk off before I had a chance to ask direction."

"Would that be an old man you saw at the bridge?"

"Yes, I thought he'd seen me for a moment as he raised his stick towards me but then, as I said, he was there then he wasn't. Do you know him?"

"He's the toll-bridge keeper. When folk used this lane there were tales of people seeing him."

"Well, I suppose they would, wouldn't they? If he's the so called toll-bridge keeper, whatever that is."

"Considering that he's been dead for hundreds of years, no. The old yarn is that one night three men, having had one too many, approached the bridge to cross, but couldn't pay the toll as they had spent it in the tavern. The toll keeper wouldn't let them cross unless they paid. Tale has it the men threw him over the bridge into the strong current and he drowned, and since then he has been seen at the bridge from time to time. They say that if you see him, you should take it as a warning. If you saw him raising his stick towards you, I would say he was telling you that there's trouble ahead and for you to go back."

"Oh, is that all? So, if we carry on up this lane, will it take us to Dungarvan?" Sean asked.

"That it will, eventually. But the road is very dangerous, especially after last night's storm. Could be trees down, or mudslides burying the lane. If I were you, I would go back. You never know what ill wind awaits you up ahead. Well, as much as I'd like to stay here all day yarning to you, I've got work to do. If you two are okay now, I'll say my goodbyes to you."

"Before you go," Becky said, "Are there any stories of a young child that walks these lanes?"

"Ah, that'd be the tale of little Betsy Malone. Her family lived in the old cottage up the lane, and one night little Betsy, sleep-walking, made her way on to the lane. As it happens, it wasn't far from this spot where she was hit by a car. It was a terrible thing to happen to such a sweet child; face of an angel she had, to be sure. She had lived no life at all. Why do you ask, Miss?"

"I think she was the reason we skidded off the lane. It was dark and raining hard when, without warning, there was this figure of a young child in the middle of the lane. We didn't stand a chance of avoiding her. But the thing is, Sean went to see if she was lying on the ground somewhere, and couldn't find any sign of her. It didn't make sense but, after what you've told us, as strange as it all is, it somehow explains these figures being there one moment and then gone."

"Welcome to Ireland, Miss - a land of mystery and tales! Tell me, did she do or say anything when you saw her?"

"It was only a split second, but I'm sure she was pointing towards us and saying something."

"Well, if she was telling you the same as the others who've come upon her over the years, she was saying: "*Go back!*" From what you've both told me, I would say you have had two warnings to go back, for whatever reason. If you're sensible, I would take heed of these things. Warnings are not given lightly, especially from the other side."

"I don't believe in any of that stuff, especially here in Ireland," Sean said.

Gilroy stood there and didn't say a word for a while, and then he said, "I take it, then, you don't belive in God?"

"No, I don't!" Sean replied.

"And you?" he said, looking at Becky.

"Well . . . yes. I do."

"So, Sean, I've told you that nobody uses this lane anymore, and the only reason I'm here is that I decided to move a few sheep today, instead of in a couple of weeks - meaning, you would still be stuck in that hedge. Now do you think that is a coindence, or just maybe you had a little Divine help?"

Sean couldn't think of anything to say.

"Well, I would say: turn round and go back. Now, again I'll bid you both goodbye," he said, driving off on his tractor. "Take heed!" he called out as he went.

Sean had got in the car, thinking Becky was following. When she didn't, he opened his door to see her standing there, watching the tractor drive off into the distance.

"You coming?" he called out to her.

She turned around and got into the car.

Knowing what was going through her mind, Sean said, "They're only words! This is Ireland. I told you, it's a place of mysteries - but that's all it is. That's the attraction of the place."

"I don't know, Sean. I think we should turn around and go home. The old tinker woman said we would have four more warnings, so I reckon there's a total of five. That leaves one more, Sean!"

"That's if you believe all that blarney. So where's the four?"

"There's the tinker woman and, although I didn't hear it, the toll bridge keeper, Betsy the child and, you could say, from Gilroy."

"So where's the other one then, Becks?"

"I don't know about the other one. I don't care. Please, Sean, let's go home!"

"But we've come all this way to find out what I've been left; I can't go back now - when in a couple of hours I'll know. Please, let's see what the solicitors have to say and I promise we'll go home."

"Well, okay, but I think we should make our way back to the new road. Gilroy said that the lane ahead might have trees down."

"If we go back it could put hours on the journey and we'll miss the appointment with the solicitor. That means staying an extra night and, as you want to go home, I don't think you would want that, Becks, would you?"

"Well okay, but drive slowly."

*    *    *    *    *

"I had one of those realistic dreams last night."

"What was it about?"

"If I tell you, promise not to laugh or say: 'I told you so'."

"I promise, Becks."

She went on to tell him the dream. When she had finished he burst out laughing.

"Ireland has sure got to you, Becks!" he said as she whacked him on the arm. "What was that for?"

"You promised."

"You saw 'Oisin O'Reilly, King of the Leprechaun's'? I've been telling you all along he's real," he said chuckling.

"Stop laughing; I knew I shouldn't have told you."

Stifling a chuckle, he said, "Sorry, Becks - I couldn't help it. So you met him? Did you say 'hello' to him from me? How small was he?" he said, trying to move out of reach of her fist. "Becks, I'm *driving*! We don't want to come off the road again!" he protested, as she whacked him again.

"I know it was just a dream, but I must admit, it felt real."

"Are you sure it wasn't?"

Becky suddenly remembered that she'd taken a photo and couldn't resist having a look. The last photo on her phone showed a dark screen with three little white dots.

# Chapter 3

"Tell you what, Honey, this hotel is a most welcome sight after the night in the car. How long before we have to leave for the solicitors?"

"About an hour. Fortunately it's only around the corner from here."

"Good, then I've got time for a shower."

"If you said 'bath', I would've been worried," he said, lying on the bed.

"What are we saying here?"

"Nothing . . ." he replied.


"This looks like the place, Sean; shall we go in?" she said, excited to know what had been left to him.

"Mr and Mrs Finñegan. We have an appointment with Mr Kieran," Sean announced.

A red-headed woman looked up from the desk and, peering over the rim of her glasses, said, "Ah yes; please take a seat. I'll let him know you're here."

A small, balding man came out of an adjoining room. "Mr and Mrs Finñegan! It's a pleasure to meet you. Please - come into my office. Can I get you something to drink?"

"No, were fine thank you," replied Sean.

"Now where's that file, Megan? Where's the Finñegan file?" he called through the open door.

The woman from behind the desk came in and went through the many bundles of files all over the room. Then she turned around and moved a bundle off the top of the file that was on his desk and handed it to him. Tutting, she left the room.

He sat there for a few minutes reading. "Ah yes. I suppose you'll be wanting to know what Mr Finñegan Senior has left you?"

"Well . . . yes. It is the reason we've come all this way," Sean replied curtly.

"Do you know anything about him?"

"Not really; the last time I saw him was when I was a very young child."

"Well, I've only met him once - many years ago. He came across as a very shrewd man where money's concerned. Word has it that he became a bit of a recluse in his later years." He continued to read the file. "Yes, your grandfather was a very wealthy man; owned a large estate down at Bantry Bay. And it says here he's left it all to you."

There was a shocked silence for a few seconds, until Sean recovered himself.

"I'm surprised my grandfather didn't leave it all to my father, who came back from America many years ago - to make amends with him."

"Not a mention of him in the will. Did they have a falling out then?"

"According to my mother, yes - over business, but all I remember is that he went off when I was a child, to reconcile their differences, and I haven't seen him since."

"When I met your grandfather he came across as a very unforgiving man. Anyway, apparently the keys to the property are with a Mr Danny Murphy. He's the local property agent in Bantry; he also owns Murphy's Bar; that's where you will find him. Well, good luck with it all. If you need any more assistance, you know where I am."


Outside the solicitor's, Sean said, "I can't believe it. An *estate!*"

"Me too! It's certainly a bit more than a goat!"

"I know I promised we'd go home after we found out, but we have to take a look, don't we?"

"We sure do!"


"So this is Bantry?" Becky said, getting out of the car.

"Apparently. I half-expected it to be a quiet little town, but it's more like a holiday resort with all the activity going on," Sean replied.

"So where now?"

"We find 'Murphy's Bar', wherever that is. We might have to ask."

The streets were full of bars with Irish music coming from them.

"Excuse me! I'm looking for Murphy's Bar," Sean asked a passerby.

"Murphy's? Yes, that would be up this street, turn left and it would be somewhere about there," he replied.

"Well, this is it, Becks. It sounds a bit lively in there. Are you sure you want to go in?"

"If I can put up with you after you've been out with the boys, I'm sure I can handle a few drunks."

"Okay, but stay close to me," he said, taking her hand.

He led the way through the crowd towards the bar.

"What will it be?" the bartender asked.

"Two halves of Guinness, please." Paying for the drinks, Sean said, "I'm looking for Danny Murphy."

"Danny is it? Who shall I say is asking for him?"

"Sean Finñegan."

"Can I ask what business you might have with him?"

"Just tell him my name - he should know it."

"If you can find a table, I'll bring your drinks over."

They fought their way back, trying to find a table away from the bar.

"Well, it looks like we're standing, Honey."

The bartender came over with the drinks. Seeing that there were no free tables, he went over to one where two men were asleep after having had one too many.

"Right, you two, as you're not drinking - out!" he said, banging his fist on the table.

"All right, Danny! To be sure – 'tis a cruel man that would come between a man and his drink," one of the men said.

"If you're not moving yourselves from this table, I'll show you what a cruel man can do!"

"Come on, Patrick - there's drinking to be done elsewhere," the man said, staggering towards the door.

Sean and Becky had been watching and walked over to the now vacant table.

"*You're* Danny?" Why didn't you say so at the bar?" Sean asked.

"When a man comes into my bar asking for me, it doesn't pay to say too much until I know what his business is. Now, you say you're Sean Finñegan?"

"Yes, this is my wife, Becky. We've come from Kieran & Donegan's Solicitors in Cork. Apparently you have the keys to my grandfather's house."

"So you're Old Finnegan's grandson? I didn't know he had one; and would that accent be an American one?"

"Do you have a problem with Americans?"

Becky nudged him and said quietly, "Sean!"

"No, I don't, but some have. Mind you, I suppose that applies to any nationality in any country, wouldn't you say?"

"True," Sean replied.

"There's a person in here who would be interested in knowing you, Mr. Finñegan Junior. Duffy! Over here!" he called to an old man clearing glasses from tables.

"I'll be there in a minute! I cannot be everywhere at once. I'm working as fast as I can," Duffy grumbled.

"Just get yourself over here, Duffy; there's someone you might like to meet." At that
Duffy shuffled over.

"This here is old man Finnegan's grandson. He's here to take charge of the place."

"What Master Calon's lad?" Duffy asked, eyeing him up and down. "I don't suppose you remembers me then? Being a small lad and all those years ago, you wouldn't."

"No, I don't. Who are you?" Sean replied.

"Hey, Danny, he doesn't know who I am! Well your daddy knows me, and your granddaddy did. You could say I'm part of the family," Duffy chuckled.

"So you knew my father and grandfather?" Sean said, excited

"I knew them all right, and that's all I'm going to say about it," Duffy said.

"It sounds like there was no love between you and them then?" Sean said.

"You ask me if there was any love between us? Your daddy and I were okay. In fact, he spoke up for me once or twice against your granddaddy; but when he left with you, the Master took his anger out on me. So the answer to that is: no. There wasn't an ounce of love in him for anyone. How could you love someone like that? All he did was take from anyone that was soft enough in the head. (Not that I'm soft in the head, I tell you. I have a good head on my shoulders; that I have.) Every week I had to go begging for my wages. All he would say was, "Remind me next week and I'll pay you," or he'd give you a little bit - making excuses that he hadn't got to the bank. He was no loss to anyone when he died!" Duffy ranted.

"So I take it he died owing you money?"

"Oh, that tight-fisted old miser surely did, Sir! So, you being his grandson, I take it you'll be paying me?"

"Look, I haven't been here five minutes and someone I don't even know demands that I pay him

money! Do you think *I'm* soft in the head?" Sean said, raising his voice.

"Danny here will tell you, that he will. Tell him, Danny!" Duffy urged.

"I'll not get involved with it, Duffy. Best you sort it out yourself," Danny replied.

"I thought you were a friend," Duffy grumbled.

Feeling rather sorry for him, Becky said, "Mr Duffy, tell us a little more about your time with my husband's grandad."

"All this talking 'as made my lips get dry," Duffy said.

"Oh, I have some lip balm in my bag you can have," Becky announced, looking in her bag.

Murphy and Duffy looked at her in disbelief.

Sean leaned over and said quietly, "Becks, I think he means he wants me to buy him a drink."

Becky flushed with embarrassment and closed her bag.

"Can you bring over what he drinks, Mr Murphy? And one for yourself."

"Hey, Murphy! We're dying of thirst over here! We could do with some service," called out several at the bar.

"I'm coming!" Murphy replied. "I'll have my drink over there, thank you," he replied to Sean.

Having refilled glasses at the bar, Murphy brought over Duffy's drink.

"Ah, that's better! Now, where was I?" he said, taking a large mouthful. "Yes, I worked for him. I've been with him some fifty years; that I have. The Duffy family has served the Finnegans since the grand Master Finbar Finnegan bought the place, doing everything that needed doing in that place. I was

loyal to your grandaddy, that I was, and he treated me like dirt."

"Then why did you stay with him?" Sean asked.

"When my daddy died I took over. I had no choice, as my daddy's home came with the job. It was carry on serving or not have anywhere to live, and work was hard to come by. I knew it would involve a lot of hard work on the grounds, but I had no choice. He got his money's worth out of me, that he did. As the years went by he changed. He went from bad to worse.

I'll tell you a tale; that I will. It was the start of the serious change in him. One afternoon I walked into the kitchen, to see him pacing up and down, looking at the walls.

"Would you be looking for something, Master?" I asked him.

He stood there looking at the big dresser. "Get your back behind that dresser, Duffy. I want to see what's behind it."

Not wanting to have to move it, I plucked up courage to ask him why he wanted it moved. To my surprise he answered me. (Normally he wouldn't.) He said, "I was looking in the library for something to read and came across a book on the Finnegans. There was reference in it to a room that had been walled up, here in the kitchen."

"Is that all you have, Master - a door somewhere in here?"

"That's it, Duffy. For some reason a lot of the pages have been torn out."

"If you don't mind me asking, Master, did you not see anything as a lad?"

"No, Duffy," he says. "I was too young to remember. The only thing that stays in my mind is being woken up early one cold morning and being sent away. When I came back my father wasn't there, and this dresser was in the kitchen. When I asked where he was, all Mother would tell me is that he had gone. And so when, I found his diary, I was hoping it would tell me a bit about what happened to him."

I'd never known him to talk so nicely to me, especially about such private things. Still not wanting to move it, I says: "I don't think Maggie's going to like having her kitchen upside down, Master."

"We'll not worry about Maggie, Duffy. We need to move it to see if there's a door behind it."

Now when he said 'we', I knew he meant me. He had me move that big, old, heavy dresser that had been there forever. I nearly broke my back moving it, while he just stood there yelling, "Put your back into it, man!" When he yelled that at me, I knew that him being nice to me was too good to be true. The old Master was back to being his nasty self; a right taskmaster he was for sure.

Anyways, to our surprise, behind the dresser was the bricked-up door. I couldn't even take a breather. Straight away he says, "Go and fetch the heavy hammer and take down the brickwork."

When the dust had settled from the rubble, I could see a door; solid oak it was, with big strong iron hinges and lock.

"Open it, Duffy!" he tells me.

Well, I tell you, the door was bound to be locked if there'd been a reason to brick it up.

41

"Someone didn't want you opening that door," I told him. But he wouldn't listen to me.

"Break it down!" he tells me.

Even though I told him that there was probably a key in the cupboard for it, he was too impatient to wait for me to see if there was. And so, with the heavy hammer and by more sweat, I takes the door down. And what do you think I saw?"

On the edge of her seat Becky said, "What?"

"Well, wouldn't you know? There's not a drop left in this glass to wet my throat enough to tell you."

"Mr Murphy! Another over here!" Sean shouted.

They watched the pint disappear in one swallow down Duffy's throat.

"You were saying, Mr Duffy?" Sean prompted.

"A steep set of worn steps, carved out from stone. I couldn't see the bottom 'cause it was so dark."

"Go and get that torch, Duffy, and be quick about it!" But that was him - impatient as the day he was born, I reckon. He grabs the torch out of my hand, pushes me out of the way and went down there. I left him to it. I wasn't even getting paid enough to do what I do, I tells myself. There was no way I was going down there. It smelt and looked like the pit of hell, but I should think if there was anything down there, they would be more scared of *him* than the other way round.

"Duffy, get yourself down here!" he yelled.

I pretended not to hear him.

"Duffy, you lazy good-for-nothing, get your backside down here now!"

"Did you go?"

"What choice did I have, Missus? It was alright for him - he had the torch. I had to feel my way down

those slippery stone steps. Nearly tripped, but saved myself from sure death, that I did. As I got nearer the bottom I could see by the light of the torch. The air down there made me retch. It looked like an old cave and with the damp cold stone walls, I would say it would be the pit for sure."

"Over here," he says, shining his torch against the walls. "What do you make of those markings, Duffy?"

"Not sure, Master," I says, "but they look like the shape of eyes. I've never seen anything like that, but I reckon they've been there some many years." There were too many to count as they were on the ceiling as well. But on another small section of wall I was able to count them. "Master, there's a group of five pairs of eyes on this part of the wall. I wonder why they should be in such a group, away from the others?"

"No, Duffy, I don't know either, but they somehow don't look as old as the others. Anyway, I need more light down here. It's hard to make out what they are. Tomorrow, Duffy - first job, get me some light set up down here, do you hear?"


"I was up at my usual time - five o'clock, to get the fire going in the range for Maggie who'd be in at seven, and, if I was lucky, I'd be able to eat the breakfast she'd cooked for me before he came downstairs. I came back from the woodshed to find Maggie had come in early and was waiting for me with a frying pan in her hands. The first thing I got was a mouthful from her.

"What's happening in my kitchen, Duffy? Why did you move the dresser?"

I couldn't get a word in to answer her.

"How did that door get there? And how am I supposed to cook food with all this rubble and dust? This is my kitchen, Duffy and there will be no breakfast for you until I get answers!" she scolds as she threatens me with the pan.

"It's not my fault, Maggie! The master had a notion that there was some secret room off the kitchen. You know what he's like when he sets his mind to something." I tells her. I can hear her now: "But why look in my kitchen, when he's got all those other rooms?"

Bless old Maggie. I was sure she must going a bit deaf as I had just told her the room was off the kitchen. "I only do what he tells me," I said, "as you do."

That was it! Those three words did it. She exploded: "I do no such thing! He eats what I give him, doesn't he? You wait until I see him! I'm going to give him a piece of my mind for wrecking my kitchen. You think, because I'm the only woman in this place, you men can order me around! I'll not have it, Duffy!" she screamed at me, banging the frying pan down on the stove. I crept out of that room and stayed away until she calmed down.

I remember the day I met her. I was just a lad. She had come to take over the last housekeeper's place as she had passed on, Gold bless her soul. My daddy said to her, "This is Young Duffy. She looked me up and down and said, "Well, Young Duffy, you see this room, this is my kitchen. You don't come in here till I tell you. Now, I can't stay here talking to you, out! " It was then I could see she was going to be a lot of fun to be around."

"Mr Duffy, can we go back to the downstairs room?" Becky asked.

"I was getting to it. I don't like to be rushed when I'm telling a tale. I was just telling you what it was like in that place. Anyway, as much as I didn't want to go down to that room, I knew I had to get those lights fixed up before he was up, or all hell would break loose. There I was down there, trying to work under the light of a dim torch. I was on edge because I had a feeling someone (or some*thing*) was watching me, and suddenly the door at the top of the stairs slams shut! I tell you, I was up those stairs faster than Paddy McGinty's race horse!"

"Wasn't that a goat?" Sean said.

"Well, there's me been living here all my life, and I thought it was a horse," Duffy said drily. "Now, where was I going with the tale?"

"Oh, I didn't know you were down there, Duffy," says Maggie, not knowing that she nearly gave me a heart attack.

"What's down there then? And what were *you* doing down there?" she asks. So I tells her what the master wanted me to do. She went over to the door and locked down the steps. "It stinks down there - like rotten meat! You got a body down there, Duffy?" she laughs.

"I have to get the light fixed up before he comes down. Will you *not* shut the door Maggie, *please?*" I begged her, knowing she would do something like that on purpose when she was upset.

I fixed the switch to the wall at the top of the stairs and turned on the light. It worked. I could see from there that he would be happy with the brightness of the light, but I had no desire to back down and see

what the light revealed. I was just about to turn it off, when the light started to flicker on and off, then it started to get faster and faster. I couldn't understand why that should be, as I knew how to install a light. Would you like me to tell you how I knows all about electrics?"

In unison Sean and Becky said, "No! Keep to the story."

"Maybe another time then? So I turned it off and on again and it was fine, so I closed the door. Then I had an idea: to see if there was a key to the door in the key cupboard. Sure enough, there were two together that didn't have a label. I never noticed them before but then I had no reason to go to the cupboard, as the master only kept spare keys there. I reckoned that might be the key, so I puts one of them in my pocket – thinking the master would be so pleased he wouldn't shout at me for a while. Breaking the door down had only broken the lock-keep from the frame, so after repairing it, I made myself scarce - not wanting to go back down there."

Then I heard his voice. "Duffy, *Duffy*! Where are you?"

I knew my peace wouldn't last.   "I'm coming, Master, I'm coming!" I called out.

"Is that light fixed up? You're just like your daddy, a slacker!"

"*Slacker now is it*?" I says to myself. "Yes, I think it's bright enough down there," I said, opening the door and turning the light on.

"Right. I don't want anyone to disturb me while I'm down there, do you hear, Duffy?"

"You won't get any disturbance from me, Master. Maggie was looking for you before she went, Master; did she find you?"

"Yes, yes, Duffy. Why is it you're *always* in my way? Get out of the way, man!" he said, giving me a shove

I watched him go down the steps, and I stood there - listening to make sure he was all right; to this day I don't know why. I was just about to walk off, when he shouted up, "Shut the door, Duffy!" That suited me, so I shut it, but I tell you I was tempted to lock it and keep him down there. Slacker indeed!

While he was down there I ferreted in the fridge and ate some meat Maggie had left on a plate for me. I know she can have a temper, but I reckons somewhere in there she has a good heart. Anyways, I'm just finishing my last mouthful, when the door to downstairs flew open and he came out in a hurry, rushed past me and went out of the room. Five minutes later he comes back in with an old book in his hand and went into the library with it. After a little while, he comes rushing back with the book, glances at me and hurries back down the steps. Now, for him not to moan at me for sitting down was a miracle. I tell you, whatever it was he saw in that book, it had his attention, so it did.

The last time something had his attention like that was when he had me build a still for making his brew. Now I confess that was work I enjoyed. We made many a bottle. After a couple of years it was good quality drink. It had a kick like a mule.

"I've heard stories of Irish Moonshine. Isn't it made from malted barley?" Becky asked.

"It's called 'Poteen', Missus. It can be made from it, but when my father and his father before him (God bless their souls) made it, it was made from old potatoes, same as I do make it from today."

"But isn't it illegal?"

"It used to be, but not these days, Missus. Even Danny, over there, has it on the shelf but it hasn't got half the kick of the real stuff. If you want that, he keeps it under the bar, but he only gets that out after hours, at a lock in. (You didn't hear that from me; I've said too much about the stuff.)"

"Duffy, can we get back to the story?" Sean asked, rubbing his forehead.

"This is Ireland; we don't rush here. Do you want me to stop?" Duffy said, irritated.

"No, Mr Duffy, please carry on. You'll have to excuse my husband; he's a little bit impatient," Beck said.

"He must get it from his grandaddy."

"Sorry?" Sean said, annoyed by the remark.

Beck stepped in and said, "Please carry on, Mr Duffy."

"As I was saying, it was the best day I'd had in a long time, what with him being occupied with his new find. I had been sitting in my old chair out front of the place, when I heard Maggie walking up the gravel drive. I knew the time by it, as she was always on time. She was one for that, apart from the time she surprised me - coming in early. Anyway, it was tea time, and she had come to get the master's evening meal."

"Haven't you got anything better to do than laze around in that chair?" she says. Not even a 'Hello', or 'Evening, Duffy'. She always brought out the worst in

me. Her remarks made me answer, "Evening, you old crow!"

"Did you call me an *old crow*?" she says.

I had to answer carefully; you never knew what she might pick up and hit you with. "No!" says I. "I said: the evening's brought out the crows!" She gave me one of her looks, but thankfully she only said:

"I noticed Mr Finñegan up by the big stone. What's he doing up there?"

"I didn't know he was up there; I thought he was down in that room. What's he up to now? I tell you, Maggie, the master's gone all strange since he's found that room."

"Well, at least he's getting some fresh air in his lungs and not breathing in the foul stench down there. I'd better get on; he'll be wanting his evening meal. I should think, with all that fresh air, he'd be hungry. Did you give him the meat I left for him?"

"No. He told me not to disturb him and I thought he was still down there . . ."

"What! You didn't make him a sandwich with the meat I left for his lunch? You're a mean man, Duffy! Mr Finnegan's been nothing but kind to you, and this is how you pay him back. I've no time for you!" she said, walking off.

Knowing how she would flair up again if I told her I ate his lunch, I called after her, "But he told me he didn't want to be disturbed!"

She stopped and turned around. "Didn't you consider he might be hungry?"

"I didn't think."

"That's your problem, Duffy, you *don't* think! I wonder if you've got anything in your head! When

you were a child it was empty and it still is. That poor Mr Finñegan!"

"Now, I may not have had an education and I might not be as bright as others, but I know how to wire up a light, and not many people can do that, can they?"

"I suppose not, Mr Duffy," Becky replied, stifling a laugh.

"Anyway, I decided to have another ten minutes in my chair (making the best of the peace I had left), when it was cut short by Maggie shouting out, "Duffy, where's that meat I left on a plate in the fridge?"

I knew I had to think fast, as she had come all the way back up those kitchen stairs to make sure I heard her.

"Come with me, you useless waste of space! I want you downstairs."

The number of times, when I was a lad, she had got hold of one of my ears and dragged me down those steps; I'm sure she would have done it there and then, if it hadn't been for my size and strength.

"So, what happened to it?" she demanded, showing me an empty plate and giving me one of her fiery looks.

"I reckon the master's hound must have had it; to be sure he did."

"And I suppose he opened the fridge and put the plate it was on in the sink as well?"

"The master *has* been teaching him some tricks."

"Get out of my kitchen, Duffy! I've got to get Mr Finñegan's evening meal on," she says to me, sounding a little bit exasperated.

"There was a particular morning - I remember it well; it was that morning the change came over the master. He came into the kitchen when I was halfway through eating my breakfast and said: "Leave that, Duffy! Go and get my big chair and take it down there."

"The big chair, Master?" says I.

"Yes, the big chair; the one I sit in every night!"

"Well that chair is no lightweight - solid oak that chair's made of. So off I went to get it. He didn't have a thought of how I was going to get it down all those steps to the kitchen and then down those steep, slippery, stone steps. There I was, struggling with it at the top of the kitchen steps and all I could hear was, "Come on, Duffy. I haven't got all day!" Eventually I got it down there, but why he wanted it down there I don't know. Well, I ask you, who would want to sit in the middle of four cold, damp, stone walls?"

"I don't know, Mr Duffy. It does sound extreme," Becky answered.

Duffy looked at her as if expecting more.

"Do carry on, Mr Duffy. You were saying?" Becky prompted.

"Halfway back up them stone steps I gets wind. Did I mention I suffers from it?"

"No, Mr Duffy, you didn't," Becky said, stifling a chuckle.

Sean grimaced at the thought.

Then I hears from behind me, "Duffy, you foul man, get out! It stinks enough down here without you adding to it." I couldn't help it; I just don't have much control nowadays. That's all I got from him, not even a 'thank you'.

Then Maggie says to me, "Is he coming up?"

51

"Don't know," says I. "I wouldn't bother him when he's like that."

"He's got to come up. I've just cooked his breakfast. Mr Finnegan, your breakfast is ready!" she calls down.

He calls back, "I've no time for that rubbish, woman!"

Now here's one thing I'll tell you: You are either a brave man or a fool to say that about Maggie's food. She responded by shouting back, "What am I supposed to do with it, Mr Finñegan? I get here early so as you have a meal!"

Now, who would you say answered, the brave man or the fool?

"From what I've heard so far, I would say the fool," Becky answered.

"That would be about right, Missus. He never got a breakfast out of her again, and I'll tell you why. When she asked what she was supposed to do with it, he shouted back, "Give it to the hound!"

That was it! She did no more than throw it down the stairs and storm out of there and never came back. I know the Master can be abrupt, but I've never heard him (in all the years I've been there) speak to Maggie like that, especially with having a soft spot for her.

And, from that day on, I ended up doing the meals (mainly for me, as he spent most of his time in that room). There was a time when he refused to eat, which normally didn't bother me, but two days had gone by - so I braved it and went down there. He obviously hadn't heard me, for he was sitting there, facing the wall that had all those markings on, talking to himself.

"Master," says I, but before I had a chance to ask him about what he wanted to eat, he screamed at me to get out, and then from that day on he kept it locked and kept the key on him; he even slept with it. He left the place less and less as the months went by, then eventually he never left that room. The bills were coming in and, in spite of me trying to get him to come out to sort them, I could do no more but leave them in a pile outside the door with a sandwich.

Sometimes the sandwich would be gone by morning and then other times it was still there, but to be truthful I didn't know if the Master had taken it or if it was the hound. Eventually the electricity was turned off. I thought that might bring him out of there - with no light, but it didn't. He must have been sitting there in the dark all the time.

And so, with no electric and no money, I couldn't do anything. The old place was just going to ruin. I gave up and left (especially as I wasn't getting paid)."

"Do we know how he died?" Sean asked.

"It appears, Mr Finnegan Junior, my glass seems to have run dry, and Danny there doesn't like customers sitting at his table not drinking, if you get my meaning."

Sean tried to get Danny's attention to bring some drinks over, but he could see he was busy with the crowd at the bar.

"Won't be long, Becks. I'm going to have to go and get him another drink if we want to hear the rest."

"Sure. I'll be fine. Mr Duffy here will look after me, won't you, Mr Duffy?"

"I'm a gentleman; for sure I'll look after you, Missus, while Mr Finnegan goes and does the important task of getting me a drink."

Sean stood at the bar and waited. Danny didn't have to ask, he just put another pint on the bar for Sean.

"Tell me, Mr Murphy - is Duffy for real?" Sean asked.

"Hey, Michael, is Duffy for real?" Danny turned and asked one of the men at the bar.

Turning slowly so as not to fall off the stool, Michael said, "Which Duffy, Danny, would you be wanting to know was real? For sure – there's two of them."

"I meant: is all that he's been telling me for real?" Sean said to Danny.

"Well now, that depends on what story it is. I've heard so many stories since he left that place, but if it's the one about your grandaddy, all I'll say is: it's been the same every time. So I'd say it's true. Why, don't you think it is?"

"Well, since I've been in this country, all I've had is a load of old Irish blarney," Sean replied.

The area at the bar went quiet. "You Americans come over here, all high and mighty - thinking we're simple folk! The trouble with you, Mr American, is you have no imagination. If old Duffy tells you a tale, then it won't be blarney, I tell you," Michael said with his face inches away from Sean's.

Turning his face away from the overpowering smell of alcohol, Sean said, "Sorry. I didn't mean to upset you; that came out all wrong. It's just, since I've been here, I've haven't really gotten over the effects of jet lag. Look, let me buy you a drink."

"Did you hear that lads? The nice Mr American wants to buy us a drink!" Michael shouted out to everyone at the bar.

As soon as they heard the words 'buy us a drink' all that could be heard was the clatter of glasses hitting the bar top and the chorus of, "Fill it up, Danny."

Sean just smiled and handed Danny the money.

"So, Duffy, how did he die?" Sean said, giving him his drink

"It was a strange way he died. I tell you, I've never seen anything like it in my life. It was me who found him. I'll never forget what I saw when I went down to that room! I had been gone from the place about a month, or was it two? Anyway, I had been staying with my friend, Angus, not far from the place. It was late in the night and we were enjoying a sip or two of our favourite brew, when I said to Angus, "Is that the hound from the Master's place howling so loud?"

"I'm not sure, Duffy," he says, "but when you hear a hound howling like that, they say it's the howl of death. I've heard it before - when old Thomas Dooley was dying; they say his dog started howling three days before. It's the bond between a man and his dog that makes them do it; also, they can smell death. So if it *is* old man Finnegan's hound, then I say he's dead. If I were you, I'd take a walk up there in the morning."

"Well, Angus, if he is dead then I reckon we should drink a few more bottles to him," I says.

"That's a good, sensible idea of yours, Duffy, one that I haven't heard in a long while. Here's to old man Finnegan!"

"I still had the key so I let myself in and called out, "Master, would you be there?" There was no answer.

I didn't bother going into any of the rooms, as I had a knowing where he was. So I made my way into the kitchen and there, lying outside the door to the downstairs room, was the hound.

"Is he down there?" I said to him; he just gave a whine. "You must be hungry," I said, going to the cupboard to fetch him something to eat. He knew what I was doing and came straight over. While he was eating I tried the door, but as I suspected, it was locked from within. I banged on the door and shouted, "You down there, Master? It's me, Duffy!"

I waited a while and, as there was no answer, I went and got the spare key but, as the key was in the lock on the other side, I couldn't use it; so I fetched the big hammer. It didn't take much sweat to get it open, as I had weakened it the last time. With the door now open, I tried the light switch but then remembered that the electric had been turned off. So I went and got the torch and went down.

The torch beam caught the back of the master's head. He was sitting in the chair. "Master, it's me, Duffy!" I called out. "You alright, Master?" He didn't answer, so, thinking he might be asleep, I put my hand on his shoulder. His head fell forward onto his chest and it was then I knew he was dead.

I made my way round so I could see him. He looked as if he had fallen asleep reading the book that was open on his lap. Now, I thought I knew all the books in the place as it was one off my many jobs to dust them. (The master didn't like dust on his books; they were his pride and joy, always reading he was.) But this book was different - it looked very old. Then I realised it was the same book that had his interest, the one he must have found in the room.

Now I'm not one for reading books, but there was something about this book that made me want to open it. So I picked it up to see what it was about. Its cover was made of thick, wrinkled leather and carved in it was the word 'Balor' and under it was an eye. As I turned the pages, I found it was full of more eyes and weird symbols and shapes with some ancient writing that I couldn't understand. But, whatever it was, I didn't like it it; I could feel the evil in it! I had to force myself to put the book down quickly on the floor. I had to see to the Master.

Then I gently lifted his head back up. I shone the torch at his face, and it was then I came across a sight that I'll never forget. His eyes were gone. It was as if they had been burnt out. All that was left were these dark, black eye sockets. I tell you, a shiver went through me, as I couldn't help having that feeling again that someone was watching me. I turned around and shone the torch, expecting to see something, but there was nothing there, other than an iron ring fixed to a big stone I hadn't noticed before. I knew I had seen something like that before, but couldn't think where. I shone the torch around the room, and the light fell on the small section of wall that the master had asked my opinion about, with the carved eyes on it. I may be wrong, but I was sure I counted five pairs of eye shapes before and now there was six. I got myself out of there quickly, I can tell you. I did no more than went and fetched Tommy Deneen."

"Who's he?" Sean asked.

"He's the local Garda."

Before Becky asked, Sean said to her, "policeman."

"That's horrific, Mr Duffy! It's like something out of a horror movie," Becky said.

"This was no movie, Missus. This was real. I've seen some mighty bad things in my time, but this . . . No, Missus, this was no film!

The old place was soon full of those Cork people that investigate cases of unexplained deaths. They was asking me all sorts of questions for hours and when they asked me if I had done it, I said, "I'm not a man that would do that! I've been a loyal servant to him - I told them so. Then they took him away and that was the last I heard from them."

Becky, who was fond of animals, asked: "What happened to the hound?"

"They do say that every day the hound could be seen, sitting on top of the master's grave, howling for him. People tried to feed him, but he wouldn't eat or drink, then one day he laid down and died. I reckon he missed his master and gave up living."

Becky found it hard to believe the story, but felt that she should say something.

"That's a sad story; poor animal."

Duffy had expected a little more response and gave her a look of disbelief that she had concerned herself with an animal and not his dramatic story. He turned to Sean and said, "So you're his grandson? I take it you're in charge of the old place now?"

"Yes, it appears so. So tell me, Mr Duffy, have you seen my father since he left with me?" Sean asked.

"Yes, he turned up many years ago. I had to think twice where I had seen him before, then, when he said, "Hello, Duffy", I knew who it was. He said he had come to see his daddy. Well, I was pleased to see him but, knowing the master was always in a bad

mood, I wasn't sure how he would receive him. He walked past me and said, "Is he in the library?"

I didn't have a chance to answer; he went walking straight in. I followed him into the room where the master was sitting and said, "Sorry, Master, I couldn't stop him." The master just stood there. Didn't say a word. I reckon it was shock at seeing him after all those years. Then he says to me, "Out, Duffy! Leave us!" Now, me being a caring person, I decided to listen outside the door, in case he needed me."

"Becky said quietly to Sean, "Nosey more likely."

Sean gave her a gentle nudge.

"What was that, Missus? I didn't quite hear what you said. I has a problem with the hairs in my ears and the wax. I don't know what's worse, not hearing or all the mess on my pillow I finds in the mornings."

Becky grimaced, not wanting to even think about it.

Duffy continued. "It was all quiet for the first five minutes, then I heard the master raise his voice, followed by your daddy raising his voice. The room was full of shouting and heated words. Next thing I knows is that your daddy comes storming out past me and left. Didn't even say a word to me. That was the last time I saw him. Have you not seen him then?"

"That's the reason I asked; he left when I was a boy and came over here to see his father. I haven't heard of him since."

"Ireland's a big place to be if you didn't want to be found. I lost a goat once, never found him," Duffy said.

Duffy was midway to taking a mouthful of drink, when Becky asked, "How big is the house?"

Duffy nearly spat it out. "House, Missus! Hey, Danny!'" he shouted across the room, "How big is the Master's house?" he chuckled.

"House will they be calling it? They obviously haven't seen it. You had better go and show them, Duffy."

"The place sounds mysterious, Mr Duffy."

"You could say that, especially with what has not long taken place there. But, if you'd be taking my advice, you would turn around and go home, the two of you."

"Why do you say that, Mr Duffy?" Becky asked.

"Do you know, Missus, I don't know; it sort of came out," he replied, looking puzzled.

Becky's face dropped. "*Number five*," she heard herself say. She gripped Sean's hand.

"No, Mr Duffy, if it's okay with you, would you take us to see the place?" Sean asked.

"Well, if you insist. I shouldn't say, but I still have a set of keys to it."

"What *now*?" Becky said worriedly.

"No, Missus. It will be dark soon, and having no electric there, you'd have a job to see the place. The morning would be better. Meet me here about 10 o'clock. I'll let you buy me a liquid breakfast, then I'll take you," he chuckled.

Sean looked at Becky for approval.

"Okay, Mr Duffy - 10 o'clock it is."

# Chapter 4

"Well, I suppose we'd better make tracks, now I've been fed. Would you be having a car?"

"Yes, why - is it a long way?"

"No, Missus, but it's an upward climb all the way to the place. I think nothing of it; I've been doing it for years. Although there was one time, after a lock-in we had here, I came out, to be confronted with a storm. There was torrential rain and winds. Well, I tell you, the wind was strong enough to blow you over, but me being who I am, I wasn't going to let a bit of wind and rain stop me getting up that hill. I said, "Duffy, the Master needs you." I put one foot in front of the other, took a mouthful from my bottle and set off. Then . . ."

"Mr Duffy, the house - can we get going?" Sean interrupted him.

"Okay, I was . . ."

Sean and Becky went out to the car, leaving Duffy (disappointed that they weren't interested in his story) to follow.

"Wow! I see what you mean, Mr Duffy, about it being uphill. What a view of the sea from up here!" Becky said.

"Ah, that cliff edge brings back to me another tale. If it wasn't for all the saints, I'd have been over that edge."

"Another time, Mr Duffy," Sean said quickly.

The car took them away from the cliff edge and on to a short lane; at the end was a high stone wall and two big iron gates, which Duffy went to open.

The gates made a creaking noise as they opened. Duffy got back in the car and instructed them to carry on. Each side of the drive was a row of tall, mature trees that blocked out any sunlight.

"Does this drive lead us to the house? It's a bit grand isn't it?" Becky said.

"It's grand, for sure; it's not far now - once we come out of these trees," Duffy replied.

As they emerged from the tunnel of trees, Becky said, "What's that big stone over there amongst all the rocks?"

"That's the Su'l, stone. You don't want to go near that stone, Missus, it's not safe. I reckon it's ready to topple over."

"Yes, but what is it?" she asked again.

"There's lots of them all over Ireland; they say they are thousands of years old, put there by men. It's a mystery how, is all I can say; they must have been big men to have put that there. I have a job picking up a full glass," he chuckled, then added, "I has a tale about that stone. When I was a lad . . ."

Duffy was stopped short before he had a chance to tell his story, as they could at last see the property before them. In unison they exclaimed, "It's a *castle!*"

"Yes, a nice little house," he said, laughing.

"By the way you were talking, I was expecting a big house, but - a castle!" Becky gasped.

"It's been in the Finnegan family since the great Master Finbar Finnegan bought it in 1860. There's a big painting of him in the Great Hall, above the fire. And hanging all round the room are five more - of all the Master Finnegans that have lived here. I know they're only paintings, but I swear their eyes follow you wherever you go in that hall."

"I can't wait to see inside!" Becky said.

Duffy put the big key in the lock of one of the two large oak doors and turned it. He pushed it open, revealing a grand entrance room of oak panelling and stone arches.

"This way," Duffy said, walking through one of the arches that took them to another door. "This is the Grand Hall I was telling you about."

"Oh, Sean, I've read about these castles, but I thought they were all in ruins."

"It was, Missus, when Master Finbar bought it, but he rebuilt it with all his money," Duffy replied.

"But this is beautiful! I can't get over it - that we own this!"

"I suppose it is, but I'll tell you, it comes with a lot of up-keep."

"Can you show me the kitchen, Mr Duffy?" Sean asked.

"Would it be the secret room you'd really like to be seeing, Mr Finnegan?"

"Sean, I don't want you going there; let's see the rest of the place," Becky said with concern.

"Don't be silly, Becks; it's only a room," he replied.

"No, Sean! It's not; I don't want you to go in there. Please, let's go and see the other rooms. Mr Duffy, please show us the rest."

Duffy looked at Sean.

"Okay, Mr Duffy, lead on," Sean said.

Because Duffy had spent the last fifty years only doing what the master of the house said, he naturally looked to Sean and said, "Would that now be seeing *the room*, or the rest of the place?" Duffy replied.

Sean looked at his wife and said, "The other rooms, Mr Duffy."

Duffy showed them round all the upstairs rooms but kept the master's room till last.

"This was the master's room, the biggest of the upstairs ones."

"You're right, Mr Duffy; it's huge. I imagine it's cold in the winter?" Becky said.

"Aye, it would be, but the old master made sure it wasn't. He had me carry logs up all those stairs to keep that there fire going," he replied.

"Where does that little door over there lead to?"

"To the tower roof, Missus; a fine view there is - from up there you can see for miles. Would you like to be seeing it?"

"Yes, please."

"You'll have to mind your head going up the steps. I'll lead the way."

"Sean, look at that view of the sea! It's breathtaking," Becky gasped.

As Sean didn't answer her, she turned around - to see he wasn't there. She looked at Duffy, and then shouted, "Sean . . . !

"I thought he was behind you coming up those stairs, Missus."

Becky rushed past Duffy and, as fast as she could, went down the tower stairs. She knew where Sean was heading, but wasn't too sure how to get there.

"Mr Duffy, can you go on ahead - it will be quicker."

Duffy followed and overtook her in the main room at the bottom of the stairs.

"Don't worry, Missus; I'll get to him before he finds the room. Old Duffy will save him!" he said, making his voice sound dramatic.

Duffy got to him just as he was standing and looking down the dark steps that led down to the room.

"Is there a light switch somewhere, Mr Duffy?"

"There is, but the electric has been turned off. Those steps are too slippery to go down without the light on."

"Do we have a torch in the place?"

Duffy knew there was one, but he told him there wasn't - to allow time for Mrs Finnegan to get there. He didn't want to be blamed by her if anything did happen to her husband.

Becky rushed over, took one look down the stairs and said, "Sean, why did you do that? You said you wouldn't; I want to get out of this place *now*!"

"Sorry, Becky. I don't know what came over me. I was just about to follow you up the tower, when I had a strong desire to see the room where grandfather died."

"Good job I got here in time! I told you I'd save him, Missus," Duffy said, importantly.

"Sean, can we go?"

Back in the car, Sean said to Duffy, "Where can we drop you?"

"There will be a few more hours of drinking to be done at Danny's - there would be fine. Thank you, sir. Will you be joining me?" he said, hoping that he would have a drink bought for him.

"No thanks, Mr Duffy. We'll be finding a hotel for the night."

"Then I'll say good day to you; you know where I'll be if you need me."

"Who knows, Mr Duffy," Sean said, looking at Becky.


At the hotel Sean had to break the silence, as Becky was still cross with him for disappearing to the cellar room.

"I told you I was sorry, Becks, but whatever it was that made me go there was stronger than me. I've never experienced anything like that before. Look, we need to talk about the place."

"There's nothing to talk about. I want to go home in the morning."

"I don't understand; what is it you're scared of?"

"You *know* what it is. How is it that I can see it and you can't? What will it take, Sean, for you to understand the meaning of 'a warning'? When it's too late?"

"It's because I don't believe in the supernatural."

"Well, I'm not sure what I believe – but at least I'm a bit more open to possibilities. Can't you see that there's not a rational explanation for everything?"

"You're not going to bring God up again are you?"

"No, but I do believe in God."

"Well, there you go – I don't."


Becky remebered when she'd first met Sean at a book fair. She was looking at the cover of a book entitled: 'Ancient Monuments.' A voice from behind the stall said, "You're interested in Ireland?"

Becky looked up. "Sorry?" she said.

"The book you are looking at - the monument on the cover is in Ireland," he replied.

"I didn't know that. No, not particularly. I'm just interested in ancient monuments generally," she replied.

"That's a shame. I have lots on Ireland," he said.

"I take it then, that's a subject *you* are interested in?"

"I suppose so - being Irish," he replied.

"You don't sound Irish."

"That's because I moved here when I was a small lad. I'm sorry, my name is Sean Finnegan."

"Becky Hamilton," she replied. "Is this what you do, deal in books?"

"No, it's more of a hobby - collecting books; then when I have too many, I rent a stall here and try to sell some. I don't normally interfere with people browsing, but not many people have picked that one up. I'll tell you what, as you are a beautiful young lady, here's my card - if you should like to see my collection," he chuckled.

Looking slightly embarrassed, she answered, "I've never heard a chat-up line involving books before!" But she took his card.

They fell in love and were married within six months. Neither of them wanted to talk about the past; they were content to be together and 'live in the moment'. That suited Becky as she'd left behind a life she wasn't proud of. She'd attended church as a child but had rebelled as a teenager and left home. Her behaviour was influenced entirely by the crowd she had become involved with and the desire to fit in had caused her to do things she thought she would never even consider. She had moved to New York to get away from that life, and the Becky that Sean knew was a different person to the one she'd put behind her.

"Look, about wanting to go home: there are so many questions that I want to ask old Duffy about the property and, if we go home, I'll never know. Anyway, I can't just leave without giving instructions about what to do with the place. Look, if it's just that room that's bothering you, I'll ask Duffy to brick it up. Will that change your mind? Please Becky, it's not every day you inherit a castle."

"Well, providing it gets bricked up before we go back there."

"Then that's a 'yes' - we're staying?" Sean said happily.

The morning came and they made their way back to the pub to find Duffy.

"Morning to you both! Is it the Irish charm that brings you back?" Danny said.

"Something like that; is Mr Duffy around?" Sean asked.

Danny looked at his watch. "He'll be coming through those doors for his pint in about five minutes. You can tell the time by him. He told me that you liked the 'house,'" he chuckled.

"I can see now what the joke was about, when we called it a house," Becky smiled.

"We didn't want to spoil the surprise," Danny replied.

"A surprise it sure was, Mr Murphy! Can we have two halves? Oh, we'd better have a pint ready for Mr Duffy," Sean added.

"Take a seat and I'll bring it over," Danny replied.

Sure enough, bang on time the door opened and Duffy walked in.

"Morning, Danny."

"Morning, Duff; you left early last night - not like you."

"I promised Angus we'd finish off a couple of bottles together. I'm a man of my word, Danny."

"That you are, Duffy. You have some company behind you, waiting at the table."

Duffy turned around.

"Morning, Mr Duffy. We were wondering if you could tell us some more about the place, and if you would consider doing some work for us? Just in case the talking is going to make your mouth dry, I've got you a pint," Sean said.

Duffy looked at Danny, "Did he say *work*?"

In a low voice so Sean couldn't hear him, Danny replied, "I think he's got more chance of milking Mrs Malone's goat than getting work out of you, Duff!"

"I saw her yesterday; she didn't mention anything about wanting her goat milking."

"Figure of speech, Duff."

"Well does she or doesn't she? Because I'll do it for her, that I will. She always makes me an apple pie when I goes round."

"Never mind, Duff; I think you had better get yourself over there," Danny said.

Duffy walked over with his pint and sat down. "Now, what would be the questions that I haven't answered already?"

"It's a question about the history of the castle. I know you said it's been in my family since 1860, but how old is it?"

"Your grandfather has a book on it in the library. I've never read it. As I say, I don't much like books, but if I had done, he would have shouted at me if he knew I had been reading them. He had a fierce temper, that he did."

"Yes, you told me," Sean said.

"As far as I know, it's been there forever. My old daddy used to tell me tales that his daddy told him when he was a boy. There was a yarn about one of the workers who fell from the tower roof when old Finbar Finnegan was restoring it. They say, on certain nights, you can still hear his screams as he fell to his death."

Having grown used to his story telling, Becky didn't give Duffy quite the reaction he wanted. "So it's not always been lived in?" she asked.

"No, Finbar Finnegan was the first, I suppose, in hundreds of years. As I said, he rebuilt it. Rumour has it that it mysteriously burnt down, but the book will tell you more about it."

"Does the castle have a name?"

"Its original name was: 'Caislen Su'l', but Finbar Finnegan was so proud of his achievement, he renamed it: 'Finnegan Castle'."

"So tell me, Mr Duffy, I take it Caislen Su'l is Gaelic; what does it mean?"

"Castle of Eyes, Missus. I always thought that was a strange name for a castle. I did think it had to do with the view, but now, after seeing those carvings, I believe I know why. Now I take it that it's light work that you would want me to be doing?"

"Mr Duffy, I was, I mean *we*, were wondering if you might be able to brick up the doorway to that room? We'll pay you of course," Becky said.

"Duffy's taken it down, now Duffy's to be putting it back up," he muttered.

"Is that a problem, Mr Duffy?"

"No, I was just saying, Missus. How much would you be paying me then?"

"I'll tell you what, Mr Duffy: what if I keep you in drink for three days?" Sean offered.

"It's a big job that; it will make me sweat a lot. I'll tell you what, as it's for you, Mr Finnegan Junior, let's say a week and we'll shake hands."

"Okay, Mr Duffy," Sean said, laughing.

Duffy spat in his hand and shook Sean's, who then discreetly wiped his hand on his trousers under the table.

Becky suddenly felt a pain in her abdomen. She didn't want to worry Sean, but this was the third time

she had experienced it since being in Ireland. Making her excuses, she said: "I have to go to the bathroom; I won't be long."

While Becky was out of the room, Sean said to Duffy,

"The book that my grandfather was reading when he died, where is it now?"

"While they were removing the master's body from that room, I noticed a ledge carved in the stone, just about the size for that book to be kept. So I put it there. I say it shouldn't be removed from that room - it should stay there, with all the dark secrets that it holds."

"Mr Duffy, if you don't mind me saying, I think you are being a little bit dramatic. It's only a book."

"I wouldn't be too sure of that, Mr Finnegan. My advice is to leave it there. It can only lead to no good for you - like your grandfather."

"Well, my wife won't let me down there, so I'm telling you: before you brick it up, I want you to get that book for me. But *not* when my wife is around - if you understand my meaning, Mr Duffy?"

Duffy looked at him and said, "I understand, but on your head be it, Mr Finnegan. I have a bad feeling about that book."

"What have I missed? Any more about the history of the place?" Becky asked, as she sat down.

"No, we were just talking about grandfather; nothing exciting."

"So, Mr Duffy, when can you start?" Becky asked.

"Maybe next week or the week after."

"As long as that? Why so long, Mr Duffy?"

"Well, Missus, it takes time to think about it; you can't go and do things without thinking about it. I have to get prepared for such a job."

"Surely it's only a few bricks, isn't it? What's there to think about?"

"Becky, this is Ireland; it's not like home. Time is slow here."

"That'd be right, Mr Finnegan. I'll let you know, Missus, when the time is right," Duffy said. "So I take it you'll be moving in to the old place? If you do, you'll need to get the electric put back on. If you'll be needing help to look after the place and the grounds, I'll just let you know that you couldn't have a better person (who knows the place), than me to do it."

"Well, if we do, Mr Duffy, you'll be the first person we ask," Becky replied.

"Mr Duffy's right, Becks; we should have the electricity reconnected, whether we move in or not. I don't think it will help with the sale of the property, if that's what we decide."

"I know I had reservations about the place, but it would be a dream to live in a castle."

"I thought you were adamant about going home and *not* living there," Sean said, surprised.

"Well, as that doorway is going to be bricked up, I feel better about it. The rest of the place is okay, isn't it, Mr Duffy?"

"Well, I've been there for many years, Missus, and apart from a few bumps in the night and a couple of doors slamming on their own, oh, and the rattling of chains, it's fine."

The smile left Becky's face. "You are kidding, Mr Duffy, aren't you?"

Duffy kept a straight face and didn't answer.

"He's joking with you, Becks; aren't you, Mr Duffy?"

Duffy, enjoying the drama said, "It's an old castle, for sure that it is."

"Another drink, Mr Duffy?"

Sean and Becky decided to go back to the hotel.


"What do you make of them, Duffy?" asked Murphy.

"He seems to be alright, but then the master was alright in the beginning. Him being a Finnegan, I should think he'll turn out like the master. Well, I have a task to do before it gets dark and one that I'm not looking forward to. I'll be back in the morning to do the glasses."

"The morning it is then," replied Murphy.


Duffy let himself into the castle and went straight to a drawer in his old room, where he searched for his rosary. Finding it, he put it around his neck, and made his way to the kitchen. He stood facing the oak door with the key in one hand and a torch in the other. Slowly he opened the door and started down the stone steps, reciting a prayer that he could hardly remember. The chilled, stagnant air seemed to go through him as he walked over to the ledge where the book was. The feeling that somebody, or something, was behind him intensified so much that he could feel on the back of his neck an ice cold breath that had the stench of rotten flesh. It made him freeze on the spot. He didn't want to, but he had to put the feeling to rest by turning around.

Muttering the words, 'Hail Mary, Mother of God,' he turned. Maybe it was fear playing with his imagination, but for a split second he thought he saw the figure of a grotesque man with one eye. He grabbed the book, ran up the steps and slammed the door, locking it as fast as his trembling fingers could manage. He stood there for five minutes, getting his breathe back as his heart pounded violently. Calming himself as much as possible, he then made his way up to the library, to hide the book. He stood there, pleased with himself that no one would find it, hidden on the top shelf behind some others. He finally locked the main door behind him and walked back to see his friend, Angus.

"You been to mass, Duff?" asked Angus.

"No; why do you ask?"

"You're wearing a rosary around your neck."

"I've been up to the castle to do something for the new owner, and being that it was getting dark and it's no place to be on your own, I felt safer with it on. I meant to take it off."

"You wouldn't get me up there, even with one or two rosaries on," Angus chuckled. "I thought you looked a bit jumpy. We'd better open a bottle to calm you down a bit, my old friend. . . . . . . . . . . . . . . . How do you feel now, Duff?"

"A bit better; I think another glass will help."

"Let's drink to your health, then. To Duffy, my good friend! So, tell me, who's the new owner then, Duff?"

"The master's grandson, Sean they call him."

"Does this mean I'll be losing my old drinking partner?"

"I don't know if I'll be asked to go back there."

"Well, let's drink to our lasting friendship and to many more bottles," Angus said, raising his glass, "and to the new master of the castle!"

"And his little missus," Duffy managed to say.

"To the master's missus!" Angus added, his speech getting more slurred.

The evening continued with them finding more things to drink to. It wasn't long before they were laid out on the floor, with their glasses in their hands, snoring away.


On the way back to the hotel, Becky asked Sean if they could stop off at the drug store.

"Why, something wrong?" Sean asked.

"No, I think I've eaten something that doesn't agree with me. I just need to get something for it." It was the first thing she could think of.

"Do you want me to go in for you?"

"No, I'll go."

As soon as they got back to the hotel room, Becky disappeared into the bathroom. She eventually returned, to see Sean trying to make the TV work.

Putting the remote down, Sean said, "Were you serious about living there?"

"Well, as I said earlier, it would be a dream to live in such a place; also it would be nice to bring a child up here - with all this fresh air."

"So you're not worried about the 'warnings' anymore?"

"Well, now that I know they must be to do with that room (after what Duffy told us), providing that's it's going to be bricked up, not anymore."

"Hang on, Becky, I've just realised what you said."

"Which particular bit?"

"The child bit. What child? Are you pregnant?"

"It appears so. That's why I had you stop at the drug store - so I could get one of those tests."

"I don't know what to say, Becks."

"Well, you're pleased would be a start."

"I am; it's just taken me by surprise, a big surprise! It's wonderful news!" he said, embracing her. "Yes - it would be a wonderful place to bring a child up. First thing in the morning, I'm finding out about getting that electricity back on. There's so much to do, Becks!"

"You know, Honey, we have to go home and sort out our jobs, and the house, before we can move here."

"Yes - if we give our notice on our jobs as soon as we get back, I reckon we could be back here in a month."

"What will we do for jobs here?"

"Well, it's just me to worry about; you won't be working now your pregnant, and I can surely find a job with my skills in I.T. Anyway, we won't have any money worries, once the house back home is sold."

"I was just going to mention that. How long do you think it will take to sell it?"

"If we get a realtor to sell it for us, it shouldn't take long. I can't see any problems. There's nothing stopping us, Becky. I'm so excited. Have I told you that I love you?" he said, embracing her again.


The following morning they went back to Murphy's Bar to find Duffy - who was busy behind the bar, washing glasses.

"Top o'the morning to ye both; it's a grand morning. Would you be wanting to buy me more drinks, or is it more questions for me?" Duffy asked them.

"Well, we weren't thinking about the drink. We just have a question: who do we pay to get the power back on?" Becky asked.

"Would you like me to arrange it for you? I can do that; the Master left all such matters to me."

"That would be good, if you could. There's one other thing we would like to ask you. How would you like your old position back, of looking after the place?"

"So you are moving in, despite all that's gone on there?"

"Well yes, providing you brick up that doorway. Anyway, we decided it would be a wonderful place to live - with our child, Mr Duffy," Becky said, smiling.

"A child, you say. I thought I had an eye to know things like that. I knew about Irene Malone in the village being made pregnant, long before her father did. It was a serious affair, that it was. I had to stop the father killing the lad when he found out. But you deceived old Duffy there, Missus. Can I think about the position at the old place?"

"Well of course, but . . .

"I'll take it," he said, not letting Sean finish.

"Well, Mr Duffy, we'll leave it all in your hands. We've decided to go back to America early to make arrangements, so we can come back here soon. I should think we'll be gone about a month. I'll leave you some money for the electricity and other things that you might need to get the place up and running for our return. Is that okay?" Sean said.

"Money you say? Would that include the money the master owed me?" Duffy asked him.

"Whatever it is, Mr Duffy, you can take it out of this," Sean said taking a wad of money from his wallet.

As they were going out of the door, Becky turned and said to Duffy, "You won't forget the bricking-up of the doorway?"

"Now don't you be worrying yourself about that, in your condition. I'll be giving it some thinking, that I will, Missus. You have a nice trip. Hey Danny, it looks like there's a new master back at the castle!" he called nto the back room.

# Chapter 5

Sean and Becky had been counting the days to their new life in Ireland and now they were on the plane.

"I know I said it before, Honey, but Ireland looks so green from up here; just think, by tonight we will be sleeping in our own castle."

"I hope old Duffy has done what we asked, and not spent all that money on drink."

"Surely he wouldn't do that, would he?"

"Well, we'll soon find out."


"Do you want to stop at Murphy's Bar for a drink or do you want to go straight to the castle?"

"As much as I can't wait to see the place, I have a feeling that our Mr Duffy will be at the bar."

"You're probably right; anyway we'll need the key to get in."

The place was busy, with the locals crowding the bar.

"You're back I see," said Danny. "I suppose you'll be looking for old Duffy?"

"If he's around; we assumed he'd be in here," Sean answered.

"Over there. I'm afraid you won't get much out of him. I said to Michael here, when you gave him all that money, 'It will be the last they'll see of that!'" Danny said.

"That he did, sir," Michael said.

"Looks as if your concerns were correct, Honey. Do you think he's spent it all?"

"We're just about to find out," Sean said, going over to Duffy, who was fast asleep in a chair with a glass in his hand.

"Duffy . . . Duffy! It's us, the Finnegans," Sean said.

"I'll be there in a minute, Master," he muttered.

"Wake up, Duffy, it's us."

Duffy opened one eye, "It is you, Mr Fissegan and his mishis. I just popped in for a little refreshment," he said blearily.

Danny went over to them. "I don't think you'll get any sense out of him till the morning."

"Do you know if he's been to the castle and arranged to have the power reconnected?" Sean asked.

"That I know. He came in on the morning after you left, asked if he could make a call to the electric company; I assume it's back on."

"Well, that's something," Becky said.

"Mr Murphy, I don't suppose you know if he has the key to the place?" Sean asked.

"Probably in his coat pocket; I'll have a look for you."

Danny searched Duffy's pockets. "These look like them," he said, taking out a bunch of old keys on a ring.

"Thanks, Mr Murphy. At least we have a place to sleep tonight," Becky said, taking the keys.


"How do you know which key fits the lock? There are so many," Becky asked.

"We keep trying till we find the one. This could be it," he said as the key turned in the lock. "Well, Becks, this is our new home; I suppose you'll be wanting to be called 'Lady Becky'?" Sean chuckled.

"Don't think I'm calling you 'Lord Finnegan', because I'm not," she replied.

"I think I'll have you locked in the dungeon, wench."

"In your dreams!" she laughed.

"I'll take the cases upstairs and leave you to explore downstairs," he said.

Becky ventured through many rooms until she found herself in the Grand Hall. She could see what Duffy meant about the eyes in the paintings that seemed to be watching you, but what caught her attention was a chart of the Finnegan family tree. Fascinated by ancestry, and more so by her husband's, she spent some time studying it.

"There you are! I can see I'm going to have to fit you out with one of those trackers to find you in this place. What's that you're looking at?" Sean said.

"Your family tree; it's interesting! Did you know that, up till now, there have been five Finnegans that have lived here? Your grandad makes six and, with you it will be seven."

"If my father hadn't fallen out with *his*, I would be the eighth."

"The other thing I found interesting is most of them died in their thirties."

"How did you work that out?"

"Well...look at the top of the tree. Finbar, was born 1826 and died 1896, that makes him 70. Now it gets interesting: Shamus, born 1853 died 1886 (33). Aaron, born 1871 died 1904 (33), Flynn, born 1891 died 1924 (33), Daniel, born 1909 died 1942 (33). That's four who died the same age."

"Coincidence, Becks. You must remember, back in those days the slightest illness killed them. I mean, to prove my point, how come the original Finbar didn't die at that age? And there's my grandad. What age was he then?"

"According to this, he was born 1928 and as he has only just passed away; that makes him 87."

"Well then."

"That's still four out of six who died the same age. I'd say that's a little bit more than coincidence and I'm not buying it that it was sickness that caused it. I don't like it, Sean!"

"What don't you like?"

"That you're 33 and we've just moved in here."

"Becks, stop worrying! I'm fit as a fiddle; I'm one of the long-lived Finnegans."

"Let's hope so, Sean."

"Why don't we get out of here and find the kitchen, where I'll let you make me a coffee?"

Sean led the way out of the hall along the passage and down a flight of stairs to the kitchen door.

"How did you know the way?" she asked him.

Sean shrugged his shoulders. "I just seemed to know. Lucky guess, I suppose."

As he opened the door the first thing they saw was a pile of bricks stacked against the wall.

"*Don't* tell me Duffy hasn't done it yet! You wait till I see him!" Becky said, crossly.

"Well, at least he hasn't spent *all* the money on drink," Sean said.

"How did your granddad put up with him? He wasn't wrong when he called him a slacker. I could think of a few words to call him and they're not as polite!"

Becks, I told you before, this is *Ireland,*" Sean chuckled.

Becky tried the door that Duffy was supposed to brick up. "Well, at least it's locked."

"I wonder what he's done with the key," Sean said.

"Why would you want to know that, as you're not going down there? *Are* you?" she said, giving him a menacing look.

"No, of course not; I promised you, didn't I? Now where's this coffee, Becks?"

"There's no milk; black alright?"

"That's fine."

"I hope all our stuff arrives tomorrow," she said.

"There's no reason why it shouldn't; meanwhile, why don't you stop worrying about everything and finish your coffee, then go and have a lay down upstairs. You need to rest."

"I'm not ill, Sean, I'm pregnant; but I must confess it's been a tiring day with all the travelling. I think I will."

"Do you know where the main bedroom is?" he asked her.

"Yes - at the top of the house.  What will you do while I'm sleeping?"

"I thought I'd explore the place; there's a lot to see. Sweet dreams."

As soon as Becky left the room, Sean went straight to the kitchen to look for the key to the basement room.  Having rummaged through all the drawers and cupboards without success, he stopped to think: *where would that drunken old fool hide a key?*"

His eyes went to the pile of squarely stacked bricks and noticed a solitary one on the top. He walked over, lifted the brick and there under it was the key.

"Too easy, Duffy!" he said aloud, putting the key in the lock.  The door gave a creak as it opened and an icy draught came rushing up towards him as he stood there looking for the light switch.

"Duffy, why couldn't you put the light switch in an obvious place?" he said, groping for it in the darkness. "Ah! Here it is!"

Sean stood on the top step, looking down.  He couldn't understand what it was that was drawing him down there, but it had a strong pull on him.

"Sean, Honey, are you still in the kitchen?" Becky shouted down.

The sound of Becky's voice broke the pull of the room. Thinking she was on her way to the kitchen, Sean quickly turned the light off and relocked the door, putting the key back.

"Yes . . ."

"To save me coming down, can you bring me a glass of water?"

"Sure."

Walking into the bedroom, he said, "You know what, I'll think I'll join you."

"I thought you were going to explore the place. What have you been doing then?"

"Nothing."

"I know your 'nothings', Sean."

"Go to sleep, Becks"


They were woken early in the morning by someone banging on the main door.

"What's that, Sean?" Becky asked, sleepily.

"Somebody knocking on the door." Sean looked at his watch. "Good God, do you know we've slept for over twelve hours?" he said, putting his shoes on.

Sean opened the door, to see Duffy standing there.

"Morning, Master. I would have used my keys, but it seems I have mislaid them somewhere. Danny told me that you're back. I was thinking that you might need some provisions, so I've brought you some milk and bread." Not giving Sean a chance to say anything, Duffy walked in and went down to the kitchen.

"Who was it, Honey?" asked Becky, who had come downstairs.

"Duffy; he's brought us some milk and bread."

"He's got a nerve! Where is he now?"

"He's gone to the kitchen. Don't be too hard on him, he *has* brought us some food."

The two of them made their way down to find him.

"Morning, Missus! It has the making of a fine day out there. I would have been here earlier but, as I was telling the Master, I don't appear to have my

keys.  Now, you sit yourself down, and I'll soon have the old place feeling like home - as soon as I get this range working."

Duffy filled the old kettle and put it on top of the range.

"Mr Duffy, didn't you know there's an electric kettle?" Becky asked.

"Well, I'll be blowed; Maggie must have hid that somewhere!"

With their drinks on the table, Becky said, "Mr Duffy, can you tell me why there is a pile of bricks in the kitchen?"

"What those bricks over there?  Ah, they'll be for the bricking up of that there doorway, Missus."

"Yes, Mr Duffy, I know what they're for.  It was a month ago that we asked you (and paid you) to do it! Can you tell me why it hasn't been done?"

"It'd be Angus's back, you see; he was going to help me, but he went and done his back in, trying to get Mrs Malone's cow out of the ditch."

Knowing what it was like to hurt your back, Becky said, "How's his back now?"

"I don't know, Missus; but the good news is that the cow's okay," he chuckled.

Becky, annoyed that she had fallen for that excuse, said: "Mr Duffy, I'm not interested in Mrs Malone's cow.  All I want to know is: when will this door be bricked up?"

"I think Mr Duffy will have it done this week, won't you, Mr Duffy?" Sean said, trying to placate her.

"I tell you what, Missus, I'm due to pop in and see Angus.  (I have a little business with him that I promised we'd do together.)  And then we'll have this

door bricked up for you soon, Missus. Now, how's that?"

"More likely drinking 'business'," she said quietly to Sean.

"Mr Duffy, as you're now back in your old position - looking after the house, is it all right that we just call you 'Duffy'? It seems less formal," Sean asked.

"That'd be quite alright with me, Master. I've been called plain old 'Duffy' for the last fifty years - no need to change now."

"Sean, if I stay here and meet the shippers, will you nip out and get some food supplies?"

"If you're sure. I'll be about an hour, time I drive to Bantry," he replied.

"You take as long as you like; it will give me a chance to tidy this place up."

"Master, you don't have to drive into Bantry. Mrs O'Ryan's shop will have all you need. It's only 15 minutes; I'll take you there if you want me to."

"That will be great, Duffy. See you soon, Becks."


In the car, Sean took the opportunity to ask Duffy if he had managed to get the book for him.

"That I did, Master. I tell you - there is something in that room that's not right. I had an awful feeling that something was behind me; it made the hairs on the back of my neck stand up. I'm sure, Master, that when I turned around I saw a figure standing there grinning at me. It was only a second but it was the most horrible sight I've ever seen. I tell you, if it wasn't for my rosary, I'm sure I wouldn't be here now."

"Yes, yes, Duffy. Where did you put the book?" Sean asked impatiently.

"I put it in the library, Master, with all the others."

"The library; there's a lot of books in there, Duffy. You will have to show me where, when we get back (but not when my wife is around). Okay?"

Duffy tapped the side of his nose, "I knows what you mean, Master."


Becky spent a few minutes taking stock of the large kitchen, but her eyes went to the unsightly stack of bricks. Realising that it was going to be a long time before they were used, she decided to cover them with a tablecloth that she found in one of the drawers. As the top of the stack had one brick on it, she picked it up - to find under it was a key. She assumed it was for the door to the room that was going to be bricked up. She double-checked that the door was locked, put the key in her pocket and made her way to the library, thinking that there would be a good place to hide it.

The library contained row upon row of old books that filled the walls from floor to ceiling. She remembered Duffy saying how the master liked his books and that it was his job to dust them, but she could see that some on the very top shelf (judging by the dust on them) hadn't been disturbed for years. She decided that would be a good place to hide the key, as Duffy obviously didn't venture up there with his dusting. She could see that book collecting must have run in the Finnegan family and, going by the many books she'd packed away in America, Sean had followed in the family tradition.

In the corner of the room was a tall stepladder that was obviously used to get to the unreachable books. She moved the ladder away from the corner and

carefully climbed to the top. Up close, she could see that the coating of dust on two of the books had been disturbed, so someone had obviously recently handled them. Aware that she didn't have long, she quickly took out the first book. It was titled: 'Caislén an Tsúil Olc'. The second one was: 'The Daily Writings of Finbar Finnegan'; but her eye went to a book hidden behind them. On it was the word: 'Balor'. She knew she'd heard that name before and soon realised that it was the book that Duffy had found on Sean's grandfather's lap after he died. She was about to open it, when she heard: "Becks! I'm home!" Almost forgetting why she had come into the library, she put the book back and the key with it, then replaced the others. Quickly she climbed down, aware that if Sean caught her on top of a ladder in her condition he would be angry.

"Ah, here you are. You must like this room; found anything interesting?" Sean asked as his eyes travelled over the rows of books.

"One or two. I can see now where you got your obsession with collecting books," she replied.

"Really?" he smiled. "I got enough food to last us a few days. It was a great little shop Duffy showed me; nice lady. I would have been back sooner, but she was very chatty, full of questions. Hey, I thought we could go out somewhere this afternoon; what do you think?"

"It's a nice idea, Honey, but I've got too much to do with the unpacking, or had you forgotten our stuff is coming?"

"Oh yes, of course. Well, at least we've got Duffy to help."

"Where his he anyway?" she asked.

"He said he was going to put the kettle on."

"I hope he's remembered we have an electric one."

"I'll nip down and see what he's up to; are you okay here?"

"Of course. I'll be down in a minute," she replied.

Becky waited a moment, allowing him to reach the kitchen. Then she climbed the ladder again and retrieved the book. She came to the conclusion that, for some reason, Duffy must have hidden it there. One thing was for sure - she didn't want her husband to see the book, so she took it up to the bedroom and hid it in her suitcase. The next time Sean was out, she would look through it.

"Coffee's ready, Becks!" Sean shouted up the stairs.

"Coming," she answered, on her way down.

"I see you've put your feminine touch on the pile of bricks," he said with a little chuckle.

"As it's going to be a long time before they're moved, I thought it was better then looking at a pile of bricks - wouldn't you say, Duffy?" she said pointedly.

"Whatever you say, Missus," he replied as the remark bounced off him.

The front door bell rang.

"I'll go, Missus," said Duffy.

"It's all right, Duffy, I should think our stuff has arrived," she said.

"Stuff, Missus?"

"Yes, our belongings from America."

Being nosey by nature, Duffy said, "Leave the door to me, Missus; it's my job to answer it. The old master

never opened it. I'll see to them; you come up when you're ready."

"Sean, please go with him. I dread to think what will happen to our stuff if he handles it. I'll finish my coffee and I'll be up."

Sean followed Duffy up the stairs to the door.

Standing outside were two men in front of a huge, long lorry.

"Mr Finnegan? We have your goods. Where would you like them?"

"No, not me, that'd be the master here," Duffy said, standing in front of Sean.

"I suppose in the hall will be fine," Sean replied.

As one of the men dropped the rear door of the lorry, Duffy was right there, assessing how many boxes and pieces of furniture were inside. He took one look and, knowing that he would be asked to help unload, said: "Master, I didn't realise what the time was! I have an appointment with Dr Sheehan for my back; it's not as good as it was. The old master had the best of it, leaving it very weak. I'd best get going; it's a long walk." And with that he quickly made his way down the drive.

Sean and the two men looked at each other. "Unbelievable!" Sean said. The other two chuckled.

"Well, I don't suppose it's going to move itself," one of the men said.

"Sean, why isn't Duffy helping?" Becky asked as she arrived outside.

"He says he has an appointment with his doctor, but he's probably hiding somewhere up the drive, waiting to see the lorry go before he shows his face. It will be quicker without him anyway."

"He *will* need a doctor when I'm finished with him! Why have you put it in the hall?"

"I thought we could sort it out later," Sean replied.

Becky tutted. "I suppose it will have to do, won't it?"

"I didn't know where you wanted it, Becks!"

The two men kept their heads down and carried on, not wanting to get involved in a domestic.

Well, that's the last box, Mr Finnegan; if you would sign here, we'll be on our way.

Sean gave them a tip and closed the door.

Becky was already opening the boxes when the doorbell rang.

It was Duffy. "I tried my hardest to get back in time but I see it's all unloaded, Missus. I think I'd better go and put the kettle on before you make a start on them boxes."

Before Becky could open her mouth, Sean said, "Yes, that's a good idea, Duffy."

"If he thinks we are paying him to drink tea all day long, he'd better think again! He's going to help move this - even if I've got to stand over him all day," Becky fumed.

"Yes, dear. Don't worry about it. It will get done - it's Ire . . ." Sean began.

"Don't you dare say: '*It's Ireland*'!" she threatened.

# Chapter 6

"Morning, Master; will Missus be coming down for breakfast?" Duffy asked.

"No, she's having a bit of a lay-in this morning. She needs to rest. That book you were going to show me – where did you hide it? I think now would be a good time."

"What about breakfast? It's all ready," Duffy answered.

"Don't worry about that; the book is more important."

"Now I know how Maggie felt!"

"What are you muttering about, Duffy?" Sean said, following him to the library.

Duffy positioned the tall steps and climbed to the top. He carefully moved the two books to one side and felt for the hidden one. His hand stretched into the deep shelf but couldn't find it. "I know I put it here; it's got to be here!" he muttered, then his fingers felt something metal. He took it out, to see that it was a key.

"What's that you're saying, Duffy? I can't hear you down here," Sean said.

"It's not here, Master."

"What do you mean, it's not there? Can't you remember where you put it, man?"

"I knows where I put it, Master. It's just not there; it's gone - it's turned into a key."

"Duffy, I know you can come out with some stuff, but what you have just said is rubbish. Books don't turn into keys."

"I knows that master, but see here - it's a key," he said, showing him.

"Come down, man, and let me have a look!" Sean said irritably.

Duffy hardly had a chance to get off the ladder when Sean pushed past him and started climbing.

"Just like your grandfather, impatient," Duffy muttered.

Sean moved several books to see for himself, "What did you say was on the cover?" he called down to Duffy.

"The word 'Balor' and it has an eye on it; you can't mistake it - it's nothing like all the others. But I tell you, it's not there!" he called back.

Sean came down, leaving a pile of books on the top rung of the ladder. "So, if you are sure you put it there, where is it then?" he demanded.

Duffy stood there, unable to answer and scratching his head.

"Show me that key," Sean said.

Duffy handed it to him.

Studying it, Sean said, "Where do you think this fits?"

Duffy thought for a moment, then said, "I don't know how it got up there, but I'm sure that's the key to the downstairs room.  I left it under a brick on that pile."

If it *was* the same key, Sean knew he was right, as he'd put it back there when Becky called him. "*Becky!*" he said out loud.

"What's that Master?"

"She found that book and the key, of course she did!  The sheet over the bricks - and she was in the library when I came back yesterday.  How did she find that book when it was so high up?  Good grief - she was on top of that ladder!" he said, alarmed.

"So, the Missus knows all about it then, Master? What will you be doing now?"

Sean knew he was in a predicament.  How could he confront Becky about the book without her knowing he wanted it?  How could he get it from her and, more importantly, where had she hidden it?  At least he had the key - giving him access to the room.

"Duffy, not a word about this, do you understand?"

"Duffy's lips are sealed, Master.  Can we have our breakfast now?"


Becky came into the kitchen.  "Why didn't you wake me?" she said to Sean.

"You needed to rest, Becks.  I thought it was best to leave you."

"You're so caring, Honey.  What plans do you have for today?"

"Well I need to get that set of keys from Mr Murphy, so that we can give Duffy his keys back."

"Ah - for sure, Danny has a spare set! I could have asked him for them. And to think I've been worrying, losing my sleep, over those keys - thinking I'd lost them."

"I'm sure you did, Duffy," Becky said, sarcastically.

"That's kind of you to say so, Missus," he replied, completely unaware of the irony in her voice. "That would be good, Master. It'a save me ringing the bell every time I goes out and needs to come back in. I'll come with you - it'a give me a chance to pick up the money he owes me for a couple of nights' clearing the glasses."

"More drink probably," Becky said under her breath.

"Do you want to come, Becks?" Sean asked.

"No . . . you two go. I've lots to do, take your time." She said that, as she was eager to see what was in the book.

"Ready when you are, Master," Duffy said, keen to get to the pub.

"Now, don't start lifting anything from those boxes! We have what we need; the rest can be unpacked later. And no climbing ladders," Sean said, kissing her goodbye.

"Ladders? What are you talking about?"

Sean realised he shouldn't have let on that he knew about the one in the library. "Just a figure of speech, Becks," he said, back-tracking.

"Bye . . . have fun," she said.

Becky took her breakfast upstairs to her room, where she took the book out of her case. She studied the front and back covers and could see that the cover was made from what looked like leather of some sort. The name 'Balor' was etched in the

leather, as well as an eye that was surrounded by strange, carved symbols. She prised open the gold clasp and opened the book. A rank, musty smell filled her nostrils, making her cough and turn her head.

As she looked at the first page, she could see it was in a language she had never seen before. Flipping through the pages, there were many weird symbols - but it was the last page that sent a shiver down her spine. Staring at her was a drawing of the grotesque face of a man with one eye.

She quickly shut the book, as she sensed the evil in it. She put it back in the case quickly and sat back on the edge of the bed. It came to her instantly. *The key! I left the key behind the books and Duffy would find it if ever he went to retrieve the book.*

Hurriedly, she went downstairs to the library and over to the ladder. Immediately she could see, by the books perched on the top step, that Duffy had already been back for it. The question ran through her mind: *What did Duffy want with the book, especially as he said that he didn't like it?* Then it dawned on her: *Sean! Had he instructed Duffy to get the book for him, or worse still: had Sean been down there and removed it?* She had to check if the key was still there. She carefully climbed the rungs once more and felt for the key. To her dismay, it was gone!

Making her way down, she went back to the kitchen and sat down to assess the situation. She had the book and Sean probably knew she did. He had the key and would know that she knew he did. Even though he had *promised* her he wouldn't go down to the room, the fact he had that key told her otherwise. She knew she had to confront him, as the worry was

too much for her. *As soon as he comes back*, she told herself.


She heard the front door close and the words, "I'm home! Are you upstairs or down?"

"Downstairs - in the kitchen," she called back.

As soon as he came in, Becky said: "We need to talk." Sean knew from the tone of her voice that it was serious.

"I'll be making myself scarce so you can talk, Master," Duffy announced as he followed Sean into the kitchen.

"No, Duffy, this involves you as well. The two of you sit down!" she said in a stern voice.

Duffy and Sean sat at the table and waited to hear what Becky had to say.

"What's up, Becks?" Sean said lightly.

Becky didn't hold back. "The key! Where is it? And before you try to fob me off, I know that *you* know I have the book, and I know that one of you has the key. Now hand it over, " she said, holding out her hand.

Trying to help Sean out, Duffy said, "You want my key back, Missus, that I've just got off Danny?"

"You know what key I'm referring too, Duffy!"

"Duffy," Sean said quietly, "go and fetch the key from your box."

Duffy gave him a vacant look.

"The box, Duffy, where all the keys are kept. You were showing me the other day; remember?" Sean said, knocking his leg against Duffy's under the table.

"Ah yes, my key box! Won't be long master."

"Sean, since we've been here you have changed."

"What do you mean? I'm still the same old me," he replied.

"In all our years of marriage, you have never kept anything from me; we had trust between us. I don't know what it is, but I feel that something's come between us since we've been here."

"You're being silly, Becks. Of course you can trust me; what have I kept from you?"

"What about when you said you wouldn't go down to that room? It was by the grace of God that I got to you in time. And now the key – which you obviously intended to use to unlock that door. Is there anything else you've kept from me?"

Sean had no defence.

"I found it, Master," Duffy panted, coming back with a key in his hand.

As all the keys in the place were made of old iron, they all looked the same. Understanding what Sean was getting at, Duffy had taken a key from the hook where all the spare keys hung.

"There you are, Missus, the key to the room."

"Thank you, Duffy. Now I can relax," she said, getting up and walking over to make sure the door was locked.

Sean and Duffy looked at each other, knowing that if she put the key in the lock she would know that it was not the real key.

"Ahahah!" Duffy cried out, making her turn around.

"What is it Duffy? What's wrong with you now?"

"It's me back, Missus; all that rushing, looking for the key 'as upset it. I'm in dreadful pain! If you could give me a hand to my room, I'll have a lay down."

"Sean, can you do that?"

"I think it will take one each side to help him up those stairs, Becks."

"Oh, very well!" she said, annoyed.

Duffy's distraction had worked.  While Becky was helping him to lie down, Sean said, "I'll go down and get him some painkillers from the kitchen cupboard."

With a glass of water and the pills, he returned and handed them to Duffy.

"Oh, by the way" he said to Becky, "I checked to see if the door was locked and it is.  You've no need to worry about it, now you have the key."

She looked at him and he knew that look.  "You said *trust* - now trust my words that it is locked," he said, firmly.

She continued to look at him suspicously, "Okay, if you say it's locked, I trust you."

"Thank you," he said with a sigh of relief.

"Well, I've got things to unpack; I'd better get on with it," Becky said.

When Becky had gone Duffy jumped off the bed.

"I tell you what, Master, that was a close one with the Missus. If she ever finds out that's not the key, I reckon I'll be out of a job."

"You're probably right, Duffy, and I'll be sleeping out in your shed."

"There's not much room in my shed, Master."

"Figure of speech, Duffy."

"So I'm not going to lose my shed then?" Duffy replied.

Sean shook his head.  "Forget it, Duffy."


Sean went to find Becky, who was upstairs.

"Hi.  Are we okay now?" he said.

"Yes. I was thinking, when the time is right for the little one to arrive, I want to have him back home."

"What - America? What's wrong with here? They have good hospitals and doctors."

"They probably do, but if he's born here he won't have an American passport and I wouldn't want all the hassle of trying to get one for him."

"Well, okay - if that's what you want; it probably makes sense. Can I ask you something? Three times you have said 'he' or 'him'. How do you know it's a boy?"

"Did I? Maybe it is a boy; we'll have to wait and see, won't we? But, thinking about it, do you remember the old tinker woman? She used the word 'boy'. 'Protect the boy,' she said."

"You know my views on that," Sean said.

"I know, but you must confess she knew before I did that I was pregnant."

"Becks, whatever it is I'll be happy, but I suppose a son would be nice."

"How's that old fool upstairs?"

"You mean Duffy?"

"Well there's only three of us in this place and I'm no fool; that leaves either you or Duffy and, the way you've been making decisions, I would have to think about it."

"Ah, ha – you're hilarious! It's a good job I love you."


That night, while they were asleep, the feeling of someone running their fingers through her hair made Becky open her eyes. She found that she was facing Sean (the way she usually slept), but she had an

overwhelming feeling that someone or something was in the room, standing behind her. On top of that, she could smell a musky, earthy smell.

Her heart beating fast, she quickly turned over and, with the moonlight shining into the room, she caught a glimpse of a grotesque figure standing there, grinning at her. In the time it took to fumble for the bedside-light switch, he'd vanished. The light going on woke Sean.

"What's up - can't sleep?"

"Sean - there was someone in the room! He was horrible!"

"What do mean? That's impossible. The door's locked and we're about forty feet up from the ground. No one can get in here. You were having a dream."

"I know I wasn't! It was real; I felt him touching my hair."

"What did he look like?"

It was dark, but the moonlight shone on him for a second; his face - it was horrible! I think he only had one eye. He grinned at me and vanished."

"There's no way out of here; where is he then?"

"I don't know, but it was real."

"Look, just try and sleep."

"If you think I can go back to sleep, you're wrong - and you're not to either."

It was a long night for the two of them as Becky laid in bed with the light on, making sure that Sean didn't go to sleep.


The months past and in that time the urge to venture into the downstairs room got stronger every day for Sean. He knew Becky was watching every

move he made; she wouldn't leave him alone in the place. He hadn't noticed the change coming over him - becoming moody and bad-tempered, but Becky had. The number of times he had to apologise to her was increasing every week, and even Duffy found that he was being shouted at for the most trivial thing. Becky knew that they needed to get away from the place as she suspected that it had something to do with it. She decided sooner, rather than later, they should go back to America.

"Honey, I think now's the time to leave for home."

"But you've got another eight weeks, if I'm right," he said, surprised.

Using it as an excuse to get him away, she said, "I want to make sure I don't have any problems at the airport, with them not letting me fly because I'm pregnant."

"They won't do that; what is it – thirty-five or thirty-six weeks before they stop you?"

"It varies on different airlines. Granted they might not, but I'm not taking any chances."

"So when were you thinking of leaving?"

"Tomorrow, or as soon as we can get a flight. That's not a problem is it?"

"No . . . but it's a bit sudden, that's all. I'll go online and see what's available then."

"Thanks, Honey."


"Morning Duffy, just to let you know my wife and I will be leaving for America tomorrow, so you'll have to hold the fort for a while."

"Tomorrow, you say; will that be business, Master?"

"No, my wife wants to have the baby back home and we won't be back until after."

"What's wrong with here? She'd be in good hands - I've delivered many cows, oh and a few goats."

"I'm sure you have, Duffy." The thought of it made him stifle a chuckle; he could imagine exactly what Becky would say to that. "Knowing my wife, I think she would prefer to be in a hospital, but thank you for the offer," he replied.

"Years ago, Master, we had to make do with who was available; doctors were expensive. I remember one night, I was just getting my head down, when Patrick Malone (my young neighbour) came banging on my door. "Duffy, he says, can you come - the wife's screaming the place down. When I got there, I could see why she was making that entire racket. Big as a horse, she was! I could see straightaway it wasn't going to be straightforward getting the young one out. When I sees this with a cow or horse, I has to drag it out with a rope attached to the tractor. "Hey, Patrick, you got a rope, I says?"

"Duffy, she's having it in a hospital."

"I have just been telling you, the Missus would be safe in my hands, Master. I was joking about the rope."

"So what was it?"

"What's that, Master?"

"Mrs Malone's baby; what did she have?"

"Triplets."

Becky came in and Duffy stared at her bump as he left the room.

"Why was he looking at me like that?"

The thought of Duffy standing over her with a rope and delivering the baby, made Sean laugh.

"What's so funny?"

"Oh nothing, Becks."

"Did you tell him we'll be leaving tomorrow and we wouldn't be back until after the baby's born?"

"Yes. We'll leave him a number, should he need us, but I'm sure that, being Duffy, he will be able to handle anything that arises."

"That's what worries me."

"Now, don't forget, Duffy, I've written our number down on the pad; ring us if there's a problem."

"There won't be no problems, Master. I'll have it all under control. You go and leave it all to me. I'll see you when you gets back."

As Becky was going out the door, she turned to Duffy and said, "Would there be the slightest chance that those bricks might be used?"

"Now, I'll try my hardest to do that for you, Missus; you go now and have a nice trip," he replied.

# Chapter 7

"**I**'m coming!" Duffy called out as the doorbell kept ringing.

Standing at the door was an elderly, grey-haired man whose face looked familiar to him.

"Yes?" Duffy said.

"Duffy isn't it?" said the caller.

"Yes, that'd be me."

"Don't you remember me - Master Calon?"

Duffy gave him a closer look.

"Master Calon! 'Tis you! The last time I saw you, you was exchanging heated words with your daddy; you left him in a proper rage. I had a terrible time calming him down. So, I suppose you've come to claim his property? Well, he've gone and left it to your son," he said abruptly.

"I haven't come for that. I heard my son was living here and I've come to see him," Calon replied.

"Well he's not here; him and the Missus have gone back to America."

"What - for good?"

"No, they went back to have the baby. I did offer my services, but no, the Missus was adamant it had to be born in America."

"Did he say when he'd be back?"

"Well, they were coming back after it was born, but he phoned about a month ago and said that they were staying for six months. (I reckon that was the Missus' decision. The master liked it here; he wouldn't have gone back, but he went to keep the peace. She has a sharp tongue in her, that she has, as I know well."

"Look, can I come in? I've been on the road for some time and I could do with a mug of tea?"

"As it happens, I was just having one when the bell rang. I can't see why not, after all you are a Finnegan."

Calon sat at the big table while Duffy made a fresh pot.

"So, Duffy, do I have a grandson or granddaughter?"

"You have a grandson, another future master for the place; that's if they come back."

"Do you know what they called him?"

"That I do."

"And...?"

"Finbar Finnegan, after the great master, but at least it's a fine old Irish name; they could have given him some American name."

"I suppose so," Calon said, with a look of disappointment.

Duffy noticed and said, "Were you now, by chance, expecting them to name him after you?"

"I don't know, Duffy. I suppose, if I was honest, there was a little something inside me that was hoping. But, after walking out of my son's life when

he was just a boy, I have no right to hope for such a thing. So tell me, what did he turn out like? And tell me all about his wife. I know you said she has a sharp tongue, but does she look after him?"

"He's a Finnegan for sure, knows what he wants. He'll do just fine here. And his Missus, apart from the tongue, I would say she looks after him. So tell me: where have you been all these years?"

"England for most of the time – working. Now I'm retired, I thought I'd live out the rest of my days back home."

"That's old Ireland for you; it has a way of calling you home. I've never been anywhere else, although there was a time when I had an offer to work up north; but I'm a true southerner, born down here and will probably die here. So how did you know about your daddy's passing?"

"I called in by chance to see Maggie."

"Maggie, oh yes; did she tell you she left just before your daddy's passing?"

"No, but we had a long chat, and she told me that Sean was now living here. She hasn't changed her ways, still the same old Maggie."

"Not a lot gets past her ears; that's Maggie (and a temper with it), bless her. So what will you be doing now?"

"Well, I was hoping to stay a while and get to know my son, but as he's not here, I don't know."

"He was asking me if I'd seen you. I told him the last time was when you was having cross words with the master. It'a be a shame if you weren't here when they got back, especially with your grandson. Look, I'm sure they won't mind - why don't you stay here? It'a be a surprise for them, that's for sure."

"You know, Duffy, I think I will. This old kitchen brings back a memory or two. By the way, what's under that sheet?"

"Bricks - for bricking up that there door," he replied.

"I don't remember there being a door there." He walked over and turned the handle.

"It's kept locked! You don't want to go down there. It's where your daddy came to his end," Duffy said.

"How did he die?"

"We don't know. All I can say is - it wasn't in a nice way. I don't think you would want to know if I tell you."

"I think, being his son, I have a right to know; tell me."

Duffy went on to recount how he had been obsessed with the room, how he had changed in his ways and how he found him.

Calon was quiet for a moment, then he said, "So where is the key?"

"You don't want to be going down there, Master Calon. Why don't you settle in upstairs? There's plenty of rooms, but then you would know that, after living here."

"You're right. That room can wait; I could do with a clean up after being on the road."

"When you're ready, you come on down, and I'll make us something to eat and a bottle or two to celebrate your return," Duffy said.

"Sounds good to me, Duffy," Calon replied.


The evening had turned into a heavy night of drinking, with the two of them falling asleep in their chairs. Calon was the first to wake. Leaving Duffy

snoring, he went to the sink and threw water over his face. "Hey, Duffy wake up!" he said loudly.

Duffy stirred. "What's that? Shhh, not so loud! Me head feels like I've been kicked by an old mule."

"You're bad company for me, Duffy. I promised myself that when I retired I wouldn't touch another drop."

"I gave up promising myself years ago. I suppose I'd better get going; there's plenty of chores to do around here. I wouldn't want you to think I'm some kind of slacker. What will you be doing today?" Duffy asked him.

"Don't you worry about me. You get on with what you have to do," Calon replied.

"How's about a mug of tea before I start?" Duffy said, putting the kettle on.

Calon looked out of the window while Duffy made the tea. Memories of his childhood came flooding back. When he came home from boarding school for the holidays, the only companion his father approved of was Finny, the hound. But he secretly played with young Duffy.

His father forbade him to play near the large stone as it was surrounded by many large rocks, and it worried his father that he could get hurt if he were to climb on them. He remembered the day that he and Duffy were playing with Finny, when he ran off chasing a rabbit. Pursuit of the hound took them towards the large Eye Stone. (They called it that because carved in the stone was a shape that looked like an eye.) The hound disappeared into the shrubs amongst the rocks. His barking led them to a small opening between two large stones.

"Wow, Duffy, look at this!"

"We shouldn't be here; if your daddy finds out you've been playing near here, he will be cross. Best we go back now, Calon."

"But Finny's in there and I'm not going back without him."

"He will come out when he's ready. Anyway, it's dark and scary in there," Duffy replied, trying to put him off going in.

"How do you know that? Have you been in there?"

Duffy was slow to answer. He had found the opening while Calon was away at school. He had squeezed through it, and found that it opened up into a long cave that went on for some distance. He had never had anything of his own before and now he had found something that no one else knew about; so he was reluctant to share it with Calon.

Impatient for an answer, Calon said, "Duffy, run back and get me a torch."

While he had gone, Calon stuck his head through the gap and called out, "Finny! Here boy!" but all he could hear was a distant bark that told him that whatever was behind the opening went a long way in. Calon pulled his head back out to see if Duffy was anywhere in sight, but as he couldn't see him, decided that he wasn't going to wait; so he squeezed through the gap.

He remembered that he had a box of matches in his pocket. As he opened the box with the little amount of light from outside, he could see that he only had one match left. Because his curiosity got the better of him, he lit the match and walked deeper into the tunnel. Drops of water were falling from the roof occasionally, making an echoing sound has they hit the puddles. Then, some way into the tunnel a

sudden, ice-cold wind blew the match out. Left in complete darkness, Calon froze on the spot. To his relief he heard:

"Master Calon, where are you?"

"I'm in here!" he shouted back.

Duffy made his way to Calon's voice. "You should have waited for me!"

"I could hear Finny, but he wouldn't come when I called him and anyway I had to see what's in here," Calon replied.

Now they had the torch, they walked together further up the tunnel. It seemed to go on and on.

"What direction do you think we are heading, Duffy?"

"I'm not too sure, but I think it's towards the castle," he replied.

Then finally it came to a dead end. There was Finny, sitting in front of a big, flat stone with three metals rings attached to it. Above the rings, an eye shape had been carved in the stone.

"Wow! What do you think is behind that, Duffy? It looks like it's a big stone door. Let's try and open it!" he said, pulling on one of the rings. "Don't just stand there, Duffy - give me a hand."

The two of them tugged on the rings with all their might.

"You're not pulling hard enough, Duffy!" Calon shouted at him, thinking that they had the strength to open it.

"We'll never move that, Master Calon," Duffy said, giving up without really making any more effort.

"That's a shame! I'd love to know what's behind there. Maybe there's treasure!" Calon said.

115

"More likely a dead body, or a ghost," Duffy replied.

Just as he finished saying that, rock dust and small bits of stone started to fall from around the edge of the stone. "I think it's starting to open!" Duffy said, panicking. They looked at each other. "Ahhhhh!" they screamed and raced out of there, followed by Finney, barking loudly.

Relieved that they were outside, Calon knew he couldn't say anything, especially as he had been told by his father never to play near the rocks; nor could he admit that he had been playing with Duffy. So they made a pact that they wouldn't tell anyone about the tunnel. Too scared, Calon never went back - leaving Duffy with his own secret place. Although scary at the time, the memory made Calon chuckle.

His relationship with his father had been distant. He would only see him at meal times, and that was only if he wasn't away on business. He knew Calon liked books and he would say, "If you touch my books they must be put back *in order!*" And that went for anything else, such as keys. Calon remembered a cupboard in the hallway where his father kept every spare key to the doors, and each key would be hanging on its own labelled hook. Normally, for a boy, a castle would be an exciting place to live, but his father's obsessive ways made it anything but. He never knew his mother as she died when giving birth to him, leaving him in the care of Maggie.

"Them grounds out there runs away with me; as hard as I try to keep it looking nice they seem to get the better of me," Duffy said.

"Sorry, Duffy, I was miles away. Did you say something?"

"I was saying the grounds needs tidying up."

"Yes, there's a lot of land out there. Hey, Duffy, do you remember that time when we found that tunnel by the Eye Stone and we tried to open that stone door in it?"

"Do you know, it was only a short while ago I was telling your son and the missus about the stones. She asked me about it and the memory came back to me. And now, you reminding me of that time has brought back where I'd seen it."

"Seen what, Duffy?"

"The stone with that old iron ring in it. When I found your daddy in that room I saw it; it was the other side of the stone in the tunnel! Do you remember we were wondering where it led? Now I know. It leads to the room downstairs."

"I knew it led to the castle!" Calon said.

"It was me who told you," Duffy replied.

"Did you? But in the castle I couldn't see where. Maggie used to say to me, "What are you looking for, Master Calon?" I always told her, "Nothing." I couldn't have told her could I?"

"No, that's for sure. But you wouldn't have found it - being hidden by that big old dresser over there. And if she had found out and told your daddy, I would have been blamed for encouraging you to play at the stone. I know my ears would have taken a whacking from my daddy, like the time you went into her kitchen with muddy boots; she blamed me for that. That old crow twisted my ear and screamed at me to get out. I only went in there to say happy birthday to her. She reckoned I called her an old crow and told her to get

her hands off me. Anyway, before I knew what was happening she had me by the back of my collar and dragged me outside to my daddy, who was in the woodshed. "Duffy!" she sceamed at him, "This son of yours wants seeing to! I will not be spoken to like that; he needs a good strapping!" My cries of 'I didn't daddy!' went on deaf ears, but what made it worse was that it was in front of her he gave my backside such a whacking that I couldn't sit down for days. I've had the strap before, but it was seeing her face, enjoying the sound of my cries, that I hated."

"We had fun though, didn't we Duffy?"

"That we did, Master Calon, that we did," Duffy replied. "Your tea is on the table. If you're okay, I'll get on," Duffy said.

"Yes, fine," Calon replied.

While Duffy was busying himself outside, Calon walked over to the door of the downstairs room. Duffy's warning, *'It's kept locked! You don't want to go down there. It's where your daddy came to his end'* merely served to fuel his curiosity. "I need that key," he said aloud.

The old key cupboard came to mind. If things hadn't changed, there was a good chance that Duffy would have kept the key to the door in there. Calon opened the cupboard door. The keys were just as he remembered, hanging on their labelled hooks but his eye went straight to one that didn't have a label above it. *This could be it*, he thought, taking it off the hook. He closed the door behind him and went back down to the kitchen to try it.

It was a little stiff but it turned. He turned the iron knob and opened the door. A draught of chilled, stagnant air came rushing up to meet him. The room below lit up as he switched the light on. The steepness of the steps and the green slime on them made him cautious – it would be fatal if he were to stumble. Slowly, he made his way down.

Without warning the lights began to flicker, leaving him with moments of complete darkness; but he noticed that, at the end of the room, was a large stone with three metal rings in it. The sight instantly brought back the memory of the tunnel and what Duffy had said about seeing the stone. He realised that Duffy was right: this was the same stone, only now he was looking at the other side of it.

Suddenly the door at the top slammed shut. It was then that, between flashes of light and dark, he saw the figure of a hideous man with one eye, grinning at him. Without hesitation, Calon raced up the stairs, but in his haste he slipped and fell several steps. As he tried to get up, the severe pain in his ankle told him it was badly damaged, but despite that he had to get out of there.

Using only one leg and in excruciating pain, he started to crawl up the steps. He glanced behind to see if the figure was still there. To his horror, it was following him and was already on the first step. Calon made it to the door and had just managed to grasp the knob with his fingers, when an ice-cold hand grabbed hold of his wounded leg and violently pulled him back down. His forehead banged on each of the stone steps causing agonising pain, until he almost blacked out.

Although semi-conscious, he could feel a powerful hand shaking his head from one side to the other, as if in an effort to revive him.   It was icy, wet slime dripping onto his face that made him open his eyes, to see that, inches away, was the one-eyed face of the horrific figure.   As he tried to move, he realised that his hands were shackled to the small metal rings and his neck was fixed to the large ring.   The powerful hand held his head tight, making him unable to turn away, and he could only look into the face of the grinning man.   The last thing he saw was the white-hot blade of a knife coming towards his eyes.   His piercing screams filled the castle walls and grounds.

Duffy, who was outside in the woodshed, heard the screams; he knew they originated from inside the castle.   Hurriedly he opened the main door and could tell they were coming from downstairs in the kitchen. He rushed down there, wincing at the terrible noise. The key in the lock confirmed his suspicion that Calon had gone down into the secret room.   Duffy tried to open the door but it wouldn't open.   Then suddenly the screams stopped and slowly the door opened. Fearful of what he would find, Duffy didn't want to go down there, but he knew he had no choice.

Gingerly he went down each step.   He instantly recognised the smell from when he'd found the master.   The stench of burning flesh mixed with stagnant air filled his nostrils.   The light flashing on and off revealed the shape of Calon's body propped up with his back against the wall, his head limp on his chest.   Duffy couldn't believe what he was witnessing. As he stood there in disbelief, the sound of metal

scraping against stone made him look up. Before him was the back of an ominous figure, scratching two more eye shapes into the rock with his knife. He turned slowly and looked at Duffy then, grinning, he disappeared.

"Joseph and all the saints protect me!" Duffy cried out. Turning back to Calon, he lifted his head and could see that, like the master, his eyes had been taken out. His wrists and neck were bleeding from marks where he'd been tethered to the stone.

Duffy knew that this, being the second death in less than a year, would cause him to be under suspicion by the Garda, especially as he was again the only one to find the body. He also knew that if he told them what he saw down there they would not believe him, and that it would cause them to suspect that he was some sort of psychopathic killer. So, like the last time, he told them nothing. He spent several days being interrogated, but as they couldn't prove anything, they let him go.


Duffy knew there was something he had to do and he wasn't looking forward to it. Having found the notepad where Sean had written his number, he picked up the phone.

"Is that the Missus? It's me, Duffy can I speak with the master?"

"Hi, Duffy. Is everything okay?" Becky asked.

"Just fine, Missus; can I speak to him?"

"Sean, Honey, Duffy's on the phone; he wants to talk to you."

"Hi, Duffy; how's things?"

"Is the Missus near you, Master?" Duffy whispered.

"No, and why you whispering?"

"I have some bad news for you, Master; it's your daddy."

"My father! What about him?"

"He's dead," Duffy replied.

There was a silence.

"You there, Master?"

"Yes, I'm here. When was this? Where?" Sean asked.

"He turned up outside the door; he said he'd come looking for you. I told him you was in America and you would be back soon. As he had nowhere to go, and him being a Finnegan, I thought it would be all right for him to stay - so you could see him when you got back. I didn't want to send him away, knowing you was asking about him. The little time he was here he seemed to have made himself at home. I never thought he would turn out a man who could drink like me; we had a good old night of it. Celebrating his homecoming we was. I tell you, Master, my old head in the morning felt like it had been kicked by a mu..."

"Duffy! How did he die?"

Whispering again, Duffy said, "In the downstairs room, Master. He died like his daddy; it took his eyes."

"Duffy, what are you talking about? Who took his eyes?" Sean said, trying to get some sense out of Duffy.

"Balor, Master. I saw him. He gave me a grin that sent a chill down my spine. The Garda have released his body, so we needs to bury him. How soon can you come back, or do you want me to arrange it all?"

"No... I'll speak to my wife and make arrangements. Listen, Duffy, if she comes back with me, not a word of how he died."

"I knows what you mean, Master; that's why I asked if the Missus was near you. You can trust me, Master - I'll not say a thing."

"I'll ring you back, Duffy."

Becky was in the other room with the baby. "Is everything all right, Honey? You look as if you've had some bad news. What's that old fool done, burnt the place down?"

"No, my father's dead."

"Your *father*, how?" Becky said, shocked.

"Apparently he turned up after all these years, looking for me. He must have heard that I'd moved there."

"How did he die?" she asked.

Sean had been aware that, if she asked that question, it would present a dilemma for him. If he were to tell her the truth, there would be no way he'd be allowed back. So, trying to water it down, he said, "He just dropped down dead; probably too much drinking over the years."

"You did say that he drank a lot. I'm so glad *you* don't."

"Duffy wants to know about the funeral arrangements. I said I'd let him know."

"Well, you haven't seen him in all these years, so how do you feel about it?" Becky asked him.

"Something and nothing. There was always something inside me wanting to see him again, even if it was only to let him know about my anger for walking out on us, but I'll never have the chance now."

"Do you want to go to his funeral?"

"Not sure, Becks. It would mean going back to Ireland, and I know how you feel about it."

"Yes, you're right. Although, I know he wasn't much of a father to you, but if you don't, I think you will always regret it."

"You're probably right. Are you coming with me?"

"Put it this way, I wouldn't stop worrying if I didn't. The thought of you alone in that castle!"

"I wouldn't be on my own. I'd have Duffy there."

"What, that old drunken fool! Well, that's settles it. We're coming with you!" she replied adamantly.

"I'll tell Duffy we'll be on our way as soon as we can get a flight."


"Welcome back, Master, Missus," Duffy said, meeting them at the door. "So this is little Finbar Finnegan?"

Becky cringed as he leaned over the baby with breath that stunk of alcohol.

"You go on in, Master. I'll get your bags from the car."

"I'll leave you to talk to Duffy while I change and feed Finbar," she said going off to the bathroom.

Sean went back out to help Duffy, who was struggling with the luggage.

"So, Duffy, where abouts is he?"

"At O'Kane's Funeral Parlour in the town; if you feel up to it this afternoon we could go down there and talk to them," Duffy replied.

"No, I'll go tomorrow; I've had enough travelling for one day. Duffy, we need to talk before my wife comes back," he said quietly.

"I'll put the kettle on," Duffy said, venturing down the stairs to the kitchen.

While Duffy made the drinks, Sean went over to the door of the basement room and rattled the knob.

"Good, it's locked. How did my father get hold of the key? Did you give it to him?"

"No, Master! I don't know where he got the key from; all I know is that it wasn't the one I has hold of. I even told him not to go down there, but then I'm just old Duffy who no one listens to."

"So where's the key now?" Sean asked.

"With the other one; I'll get it for you," Duffy said, getting up from the table.

"No . . . not now, you fool!" The words were out and he was embarrassed. He had heard his wife call Duffy that so much that he had begun to use the term. "No, you finish your tea. Tell me more about my father; what was he like?"

"He said he had been living in England all this time and decided that, as he had retired, he wanted to come back home to spend the rest of his years, and, I suppose, make things all right with you. I told him he was a granddaddy and the child's name. I think he was looking forward to seeing you and the family."

"Was he still drinking?"

"No. He said the day he retired he had given it up, that was apart from just the one time the night before he died - we opened a bottle or two. But that had nothing to do with him going down there, Master. I wouldn't want you blaming the old *fool* for that," he said looking Sean in the face.

Realising he had hurt his feelings, Sean said, "You're not an old fool, Duffy. I'll not blame you.

Now, remember what I told you - not a word about it to my wife."

"What's that about your wife, Sean?" Becky said, coming through the door with the baby.

"I was telling Duffy that my wife won't be pleased that the door hasn't been bricked up, and that, if he hadn't been drinking tea all day while we were away, it might have got done."

Duffy choked on his tea, "Well, I . . ."

"Don't say a word, Duffy. In fact, don't bother yourself with it. Tomorrow I'll find some people who are reliable and not too lazy to do the job. And, yes - I will have a cup of tea, Duffy," Becky said, fondling the baby.

# Chapter 8

"Morning, Duffy. I'll be ready to leave in ten minutes."

"I'll be ready, Master."

While waiting for the baby to wake, Becky got out her laptop and searched for builders. Several names and phone numbers came up of firms that were based in Bantry. Having written them down, she had the idea of searching for someone who was an authority on Irish castles. Professor Michael Kegan, based in Cork, came up on the screen. Cork was about an hour's drive away and she was hoping to find someone a little closer, as she didn't want to leave the baby that long with Sean, but nothing else came up. Having shut the computer down, she remembered the book on the top shelf in the library.

She looked over at Finbar and saw that he was sound asleep in his basket. She didn't want to leave him, but she knew she would have to get it before her husband came home. She could have asked Sean to get it for her, but it would bring up the touchy subject

of her thinking there was something spooky going on, and him being defensive of the place. She decided that, if she left all the doors open, she would hear Finbar if he should wake, and as it would only take five minutes, it would be all right.

Her timing was spot on; she walked back into the room just as Finbar stirred.

"Well, good morning! I suppose you want feeding," she said, picking him up.



"My name's Finnegan. I've come about my father's burial," Sean said to one of the parlour directors.

"Mr Finnegan, good morning to you. First of all, may I offer my condolences to you for your loss. We have him in the other room; would you like to see him?"

Sean was unprepared for the question. Half of him wanted to and the other didn't. Remembering how he'd met his end, he didn't think he could cope with the sight.

"No, thank you. I don't think I could."

The director, who was used to the reaction of people who'd lost love ones in unsightly ways, said, "Mr Finnegan, we pride ourselves on preparing the deceased so their loved ones can pay their last respects. I can assure you he will look just as if he is asleep, if that helps you."

"If you don't mind me saying, Master, you should see your daddy. I'm sure there are a few words that you might be wanting to say to him, especially after all these years," Duffy spoke up.

"Just five minutes then," Sean said.

"You take as long as you like, Mr Finnegan; just come out when you are ready," the director replied.

Sean went into the small, darkened room. He wished he had Becky by his side, as she was when he went to see his mother when she died. Slowly he approached the coffin and looked in. The director was right; he looked just as if he was asleep. He was dressed smartly in a suit and tie. Sean had rehearsed many times the angry words he would say to his father, but now it didn't matter. All that came to him were the good times when he was a small boy, before his father had taken to drink.

"Why couldn't you have stayed alive a bit longer, so you could have seen your grandson? Now he's going to grow up, not knowing his granddad - as I did!" he said, getting upset. He stood there a little while looking at him, and then said, "I forgive you, Dad," and with that he bent over and kissed his forehead and made his way out.

"So, Mr Finnegan, shall we go into the office?" the director said, leading the way.


"How did it go, Honey?" Becky asked.

"Fine. You'll be pleased to know I made my peace with him."

Becky gave him a hug. "I'm so pleased. When's the funeral?" she asked.

"Well the undertakers said they can do it for Thursday, but that depends on Father Dorian. I've made an appointment to see him tomorrow, at Finbar's Church. According to Duffy, it's where all the Finnegans are buried."

"By the sound of it, Finbar's quite a common name, but I just love it," Becky said.

"I know you do – or you wouldn't have chosen the name for our son."

"So who was Finbar?" Becky asked.

"You know, Becky, that's one thing I love about you. You give me plenty of opportunities to show off my knowledge about Ireland."

"That's because I'm proud of you, Honey."

"I only know what I read about him. He was the son of an artisan and a lady of the Irish royal court. Born in Connaught, Ireland, he was educated at Kilkenny, where the monks named him 'Fionnbharr'."

"What does that mean?" she asked.

"I looked that up: 'White Head', because of his light hair. He lived as a hermit on a small island at Lough Eiroe, and then founded a monastery on the River Lee that developed into the city of Cork, of which he was the first bishop. Apparently many miracles are attributed to him, and they say the sun didn't set for two weeks after he died at Cloyne about the year 633."

"And we named our son after him," Becky said.

"Yeah, but being a boy, I don't suppose for one minute he's going to be a little saint growing up," Sean chuckled.

"You leave him alone! When I look at him asleep, he's a little saint to me," she replied.

"So how's he been?"

"So good - sleeping most of the time, as they do. By the way, I found two builders in the town. I'm give them a ring this afternoon and see if one of them can make a start this week."

"You'll be lucky! I don't know what all the urgency is for; it's not as if the door is unlocked, and I can't see it being so, especially as you have the key," Sean replied.

Because Becky was expecting a bit more of an encouraging answer from him, her suspicions were aroused again.

"Where's Duffy?" she asked.

"I dropped him off at the pub, to ask Mr Murphy if the wake could be held there."

"I take it that was his idea?" she said.

"As it happens it was mine. I know I didn't really know my father, but I felt it was something that he would have liked. I wanted to give him a good send off. Why, do you object to me giving my father a wake?" Sean said, irritably.

"No, sorry. I thought it was that old fool suggesting it for an excuse to get drunk. I couldn't be pleased enough for you about your father."

"Sorry, Becks. I didn't mean for it to come out like that; I don't know what came over me. I suppose it must have been seeing him after all these years and the fact that he's dead."

"Would you like me to come with you tomorrow to see the priest?

"You have enough to do with Finbar," Sean replied.

"Honestly Honey, he's no problem at all. He'll be sleeping most of the time, and anyway I want to."

"If you're sure. We have to be there by 10.30."

"10.30 it is then," Becky said.

Becky could see Sean looking at his watch and getting agitated with her as she was getting Finbar out of the car.

"Becks, I don't want to be late. Apparently (according to the undertakers), Father Dorian doesn't like to be kept waiting."

Becky kept herself from saying, "If you helped me, we wouldn't be late," as she knew it wasn't the normal Sean speaking.

"Right, let's get going," she said and started pushing the buggy up the church path. Becky was interested in old churches and asked, "How old is this place?"

"I'm not sure, but I think 1800s. Some of those gravestones look very old; they've probably got dates on them, but we haven't got time to look right now."

Standing at the entrance of the church was a white-haired old man and, by his dog collar, Becky knew he must be Father Dorian.

"You must be Sean, and I take it this is your wife?" he asked, looking her up and down.

"Yes, Becky and our son, Finbar. I'm sorry if we're late," Sean said, contritely.

Father Dorian looked at his watch and said, "You're on time - just! Shall we go into the vestry?" he said, walking off into the church.

"I have spoken to O'Kane's Funeral Parlour and they tell me that your father died in an unexplained manner. Can you tell me more?" Father Dorian asked.

"I'm not too sure what you mean by 'unexplained manner'. I assumed it was the drink that killed him," Sean replied.

Becky's ears pricked up when she heard the word 'unexplained'.

"If I'm not mistaken, your granddaddy - his death was unexplained too. I hear they both died at the castle. Is that true?" Father Dorian asked.

Sean realised that this would cause problems for him, as he had told Becky his father died from drinking; now he knew he would have to answer the question carefully.

"I only know what Duffy told me," he said, and deliberately tried changing the subject. "Do you know Duffy; he works at the castle?" Sean asked him.

"I know Duffy and I knew his father. Both heathens; their God is their drink. But we're not here to discuss the lies of Duffy. I told O'Kane's Thursday 3 o'clock sharp would be fine. Are there any hymns or readings you would like?" Father Dorian asked.

"I don't know, you see I didn't really know him; I haven't seen him since I was a child. Did you know him, Father?"

"Yes - when he was a young lad, before his father sent him to boarding school. You Finnegans all come back eventually. I have them all in the graveyard outside."

"Have you? I'd like to see their gravestones," Becky said.

Father Dorian gave her an unamused look. "As you don't know what you would like in the way of hymns, would you like me to arrange it? Mrs Flanagan can play most things on the organ, and meanwhile you can make your mind up about saying a few words (as long as they are short). I have a mass at 4.30 and I wouldn't want to run over."

Looking at his watch again, he said, "Well, I'll see you Thursday at 3 o'clock."

He saw them out to the path.

"By the way, the child - I take it that's he's going to be baptized, and then confirmed when he's older?"

"Yes, Father Dorian," Sean replied.

"Good! There's too many young heathens running around nowadays," he said.

As Becky got into the car, she asked Sean, "Why did you say that, when Finbar's not going to be Catholic?"

"I took it that he was going to be, as all the Finnegans were," he replied.

"Well *you* weren't; you're not the slightest bit religious," Becky said.

"That may be so, but I had to say that to keep him happy; you could see that he was a bundle of fun. But I think it would be nice for Finbar when he comes of age."

"We'll discuss it when we get home - along with how your father really died," Becky announced.


Back at the castle, Becky said, "Will you find that Duffy for me. I need to ask him some questions."

Sean agreed, as he wanted to warn him that she was going to question him about the death of his father. He thought he knew where Duffy would be; if it wasn't his woodshed it would be Murphy's Bar, and if it was the latter he would have no choice but to wait till he came back.

"Duffy, you in here?" Sean called out, opening the door of the shed. He could see that he wasn't, but as

he turned around to go back in, he could see him staggering up the drive.

"Duffy, you were supposed to look after the place while we were out, not disappear to Murphy's!"

"I had a terrible thirst, Master, from chopping up all that wood, that I did," he replied.

"What's wrong with water? There's plenty of it inside," Sean said.

"Water! Master, I hasn't touched water in years; full of germs to be sure."

Sean could see he wasn't getting anywhere, and said, "My wife wants to see you."

As drunk as he was, the mention of the Missus made him say, "I done nothing wrong, Master. I'm sure I haven't; it will be those bricks. I will get it done!"

"Well, she might bring that up, but she wants to ask you about how my father died. Do you remember we agreed to tell her, if she asked, that it was drink?"

"Did we?" he replied, thinking about it.

"Yes, Duffy! Please say you do; otherwise I'll be joining you in the woodshed for the night and then I'll be on a plane home."

"That's my shed," he muttered, staggering towards the front door.

Sean went on ahead to tell Becky that he'd found Duffy and that, because he had been drinking, he was probably unlikely to remember much.

Duffy staggered down the stairs into the kitchen. "You wanted to see me, Mis-sh-es?"

Becky could see that she wasn't going to get any sense out of him, and said, "The morning will do. Sean, take him out to his shed - he can sleep it off out there. Otherwise his breath will stink the place out."

"Come on, Duffy, let's get you to the shed."

Becky picked up the phone. "Good morning, is that O'Sullivan's Builders?"

"That'd be me at your service, what can I do for you?"

"I have a doorway that needs bricking up. Do you undertake small jobs like that?"

"Yes, Mam, that I do."

"Good, when could you do it?"

"Now let me see, when was you thinking of it to be done?" he replied. "Tomorrow! No, Mam, I'm booked up for at least four weeks; I could do it then."

Becky knew she would have to offer an incentive to make it happen, knowing how hard it was to get anything done quickly in Ireland.

"Mr O'Sullivan, if you do it tomorrow, I'll pay you twice as much as you would normally charge and all the bricks are here."

"You say twice as much? As it happens, I think I can juggle some jobs around. I'll be seeing you in the morning." he replied.

"Mr O'Sullivan, by the way, how much do you normally charge?"

"Don't let us worry too much about that. Let's say you will get a fine job done for your money, that's for sure. I has a reputation to keep up and I'm honest. I'll see you in the morning," with that he put the phone down.

"Mr O'Sullivan, you haven't even ask where I live," she said looking at the phone. "Is everyone here like Duffy?" she said, redialling. "Mr O'Sullivan, it's Mrs Finnegan here."

"Who's that?"

". . . about the doorway that needs bricking up?"

"That's strange - I was just talking to someone else about a bricking up of a doorway."

"Yes that was me. You hung up without asking my name or address.

"That I did! Just as well you phoned back; I would have set off tomorrow, not having a clue where I was going,' he chuckled.

Becky gave him all the details and made him repeat them to her, but judging by the conversation they'd just had, she seriously doubted he would turn up.

"Morning, Missus. The master tells me you wanted words with me."

"Yes, Duffy, I do. Tell me how my husband's father died, and where."

Duffy thought and then said, "Would that be Master Calon Finnegan?"

"Yes . . . *my husband's father.*" Becky knew he was playing for time to think about what to say. She said, "Let me spell it out for you: *how did he die and where?*"

"Shall I put the kettle on?"

"No! I'm going to ask one more time and then that's it - you leave!" Becky said, raising her voice.

Duffy stood with a vacant look on his face.

"Well?" Becky said.

"Well what, Missus?"

"What do mean '*well what*'?" she said, becoming irate.

"I'm waiting for you to ask me, so I can leave; I has lots of things to do outside."

Becky couldn't make up her mind whether he was playing the fool, or whether he really was one. She decided she would take a more gentle approach with him.

"Duffy, please sit down. All I want to know is about Master Calon, who was here a little while ago. You remember him don't you?" she said patiently.

"Yes, Missus; I knows Master Calon."

"Good. Now I want you to think about it very carefully before you answer. You remember you phoned us and said that he had died? Well, I'm asking: *how* did he die?" Becky said, speaking as slowly and clearly as she could.

Duffy sat there giving her the impression that he was doing as she had asked - thinking carefully; but really he was hoping that the master would come and rescue him. However, realising that wasn't going to happen, he knew he couldn't win. If he didn't say anything, he would be out of a home and job, and if he *did,* the master might throw him out. Reluctantly, he said very quickly: "He died the same way as his father - down there."

"Whoa! *What did you say*? Repeat it slowly," she told him.

"Master Calon died down there in that room," Duffy said, looking down at the table rather than at her.

"Are you saying: *he died down in that room and the same way as his father*?"

"That would be about what I'm saying, Missus," Duffy said, now looking at her.

"Tell me one more thing, Duffy. Does my husband know that?"

Sheepishly, he replied, "That he did, Missus. I did tell him on the phone."

Becky sat there not saying a word.

"Can I go now, Missus?" Duffy asked.

"Yes, you can go. If you see my husband outside with Finbar, send him to me."

"I will do that for sure, Missus," he replied.

"Oh, by the way, Duffy, do you have a brother who's a builder?"

"I has a brother - Casey, that I do; but he's not a builder. He got himself a education and has a fine job as one of them postmans in Cork. I haven't seen him in years, but I have a cousin, Pat, who might be; he was always good at that sort of stuff. Why, Missus, do you have something to build? I could always get hold of him for you. Or, if you tell me what it is, I could do it."

"No. Don't worry, Duffy; it's all taken care of. That will be all, but don't forget about my husband."

"Rest assured, Missus, you can rely on me not to forget."


It wasn't long before Sean came into the kitchen carrying Finbar.

"We had a wow of a time, Mom," Sean said.

"I bet he slept all the time," she replied. "You got my message from Duffy then?"

"No, what message?"

"Did you see him?"

"Yes - he stuck his head in the buggy, grinning and making cooing noises at Finbar."

"And he didn't say anything to you?"

"No, why - should he have?"

"Never mind. I should have remembered: his name is Duffy. I've had words with him, and I didn't like what he told me, Sean."

The only time she called him by his name was if it was serious. "What's up now?" he said, in a tone that told her he was getting tired of the inquisitions.

"You told me your father died because of drink, but Duffy told me otherwise. He said he died the same way of as his father. You've lied to me again, Sean. Why?" she said, starting to cry.

Sean sat down next to her, and put his arm around her.

"I didn't want to, Becks, but if I had told you the truth, you wouldn't have come back here, or let me come on my own to bury my father, would you?"

"Put yourself in my place. If someone told you that your wife would be in danger if she  stayed here, and you'd seen evidence of that happening, you would take her as far away as possible wouldn't you?" she replied.

"But, Becks, you can't give up all this because of a few scaremongering words."

"How can you say that when there have already been two unexplained deaths down in that room? If you don't care about me, then care about Finbar. The old lady told me to protect him. I know, at the time, it didn't make sense - because I didn't know I was pregnant, but now he's been born, it all makes sense. And I feel, if we stay here, I won't be able to protect him (or you), especially with you being drawn to that room and lying to me."

"What about if I get the priest to come here and do one of those things that they do when there's

something going on in a place. What's it called?" he said, trying to think of the term.

"Exorcism," Becky replied.

"That's it - an exorcism. That will do it; then you'll have nothing to worry about."

Becky thought about it for a few moments.

"Okay. This is how it's going to go: you arrange for him to come. I had organised a builder to come tomorrow and brick the door up while we're at the funeral. But thinking about it, all that would do is contain whatever it is in there. I'll cancel him until Father Dorian's done the exorcism."

"Surely then there won't be any need to brick the door up?" Sean suggested.

"It's getting bricked up or we're leaving this place for good!" she replied, firmly.

"Ok, I'll talk to him tomorrow, Becky!"

"Good!"

# Chapter 9

"They were fine words you said about your daddy, Sean."

Sean turned to see a once redheaded, but now mostly grey, elderly lady.

"You don't remember me, do you? I'm Maggie. I used to look after you before your daddy took you away.'

"Sorry, I don't, but I have heard about you from Duffy,' Sean replied.

"Yes, I heard he was back at the place; I would say working for you, but something tells me he'll still be spending most of his time either at the pub or drinking tea," she said.

"That sounds like Duffy," Sean laughed.

"Talking about him, where is he? I still haven't forgiven him for wrecking my kitchen."

"He was here, but I suspect (because I left him to organise my father's wake) he's probably gone to Mr Murphy's bar to make sure he's ready for us."

"That's the only time that man moves himself - when there's drink involved," Maggie said.

"You are coming aren't you? Everyone is welcome."

"Well if I do, it will just be for a little one - as it's your father."

"Good. You haven't met my wife, Becky, and my son, Finbar?" Sean said, looking over to where Becky was chatting with the priest.

"No, but I heard that you had a wife and son."

Seeing that Becky needed rescuing from Father Dorian, Sean called out, "Sorry, Father, there's someone over here who would like to meet my wife."

Becky walked over. "I thought I'd never get away from him! I've had ten minutes of him lecturing me on the subject of confirmation of children, and trying to convert me to being a Catholic."

"Do you remember Duffy telling us about Maggie? Well, here she is! Maggie, this is my wife, Becky and Finbar," Sean said. "Can I leave you with Maggie? I just want to thank Father Dorian for the service."

"Yes, that's fine. Don't forget to talk to him about you-know-what."

"Yes, okay," he replied and started walking over to him.

"Hello, my dear, and hello to you, young master," Maggie said, stroking his cheek. "How do you like it here? And what about the castle - it's a fine place, isn't it?" Maggie asked Becky.

"Ireland's a beautiful place, and the castle, well it's big and full of character and mystery," Becky said, searching for words.

"I would agree with the word 'character', but having worked there for a very long time, I've never noticed any mystery about the place - only what was going on in Duffy's head," Maggie chuckled. "I would offer to

come and housekeep for you but I'm afraid the castle has had the best of me, walking up and down that hill twice a day and, at my age, I have a job with my own little cottage. If you know what I mean dear."

"Of course; but it's kind of you to offer. Are you coming back for food and drink?"

"Yes, Sean has already asked me."

Maggie noticed that Becky kept looking over at Sean in conversation with Father Dorian.

"Everything all right, my dear? You have the look of a woman with troubles on her mind. Am I right?"

Becky had longed to find someone she could chat with about her concerns and decided that maybe Maggie was the one.

"Maggie, do you know much about the castle and what's gone on there?"

"I'm not too sure what you mean, dear; if you could give me a little more on the subject, I might be able to help."

Becky knew she didn't have long to tell Maggie what was worrying her. She didn't want Sean to know that she had been talking to anyone about it, so she quickly explained what had happened.

"Well my dear, I remember the day when I first saw that doorway. To think - all those years it had been there behind that old dresser, and I didn't know! But then it was a surprise to everyone, including that good-for-nothing Duffy. I *did* notice the change taking hold of Mr Finnegan after that door had been uncovered. He could be a little awkward at times, but I knew how to handle him. At the end, he had completely changed. It wasn't the Mr Finnegan I first knew."

"Oh, Maggie, that's what is happening to Sean! Since we've been here we've never rowed so much and he lies to me, which he has never done before," Becky replied.

"Has he been down in that room?"

"That's the thing; I don't really know. I got to him once, just in time. He says that he feels a compulsion to go down there, but I keep it locked now and I've hidden the key. It was supposed to be bricked up today (while we were here), but Sean said that he would ask Father Dorian to perform an exorcism down there - which makes sense, before it's bricked up. That's what I hope he's talking to him about now."

"Now I can see why you have that anxious look on your face, my dear. I would keep an eye on him. I'm sorry I can't tell you any more about the place, or be of more help," Maggie said, patting Becky's arm.

"Thanks, Maggie; it has helped - speaking to someone about it."

Maggie walked off, then stopped and turned back.

"My dear, look here's my number. If ever you need me, or just want to talk, give me a ring."

"Thank you, Maggie, I will."


"Thank you, Father Dorian, for the service. "Will you be coming to the wake?" Sean asked.

"I'm afraid I have a Communion Service in about twenty minutes, but once it's over I dare say I could spare time for a glass or two. I take it it's at Murphy's?"

"Yes; I suspect it will be going on for some time. I'll look forward to seeing you there then." Sean was just about to walk away when he stopped and said, "I

nearly forgot - I need to ask you something, but I'm not to sure where to start."

"Well, you'd better start somewhere - I haven't got long!" Father Dorian said, looking at his watch.

"It's my wife, Becky; she's concerned that we have a problem at the castle. There's a room that has been uncovered by my grandfather in the basement and she thinks that there's something down there that caused the deaths of both him and his son. I told her that she's being silly but she won't stop worrying about it. She thinks that whatever it is will take me as well; so, to appease her, I said I'd have a word with you. I wondered if you would come to the castle and have a look down there."

"Now that I know that both of them met their end at the castle, it's my opinion that your wife may not be as silly as you think." He noticed that Becky was looking at them. "I'll try and call by next week. Do I have a number for you?"

Sean gave him the number, then left with Becky to go to Murphy's.

"Did you speak to the priest about the basement room?" Becky asked him.

"Yes. I *said* I would, didn't I?" Sean replied, sounding annoyed.

"Sean! I only asked," she said, upset by his tone.

They didn't say a word to each other all the way back to Murphy's Bar.

"I'm not coming in. You can go ahead, and I'll go home with Finbar; try not to be too late."

"How am I supposed to get back if you take the car?" he asked.

"You can walk back with that Duffy and hopefully you'll be in a better mood. I'll probably be asleep when you get in, so don't make a noise."

She left him standing there, watching her drive off. He shrugged his shoulders and went into the bar.

"Over here, Master!" Duffy called out. "Danny, let's have a half over here, so the master can toast his daddy!"

"No, Duffy, make it a large one - I need it."

"You heard the master, Danny. Large ones they are!" Duffy called over.

Sean sat down at the table with Duffy and a few others he didn't know.

"No Missus, Master?"

"No, Duffy. She's a little tired and has gone home," he said, as an excuse for her absence.

Looking around, Sean noticed that the bar was extra busy with people he hadn't seen before.

"Did all these people know my father?" he asked Duffy.

"That I don't know, Master, but when word gets out there's a wake, they turn up to pay their respects and give him a good send off."

Sean suspected the real reason was that there were free drinks and that he would probably be paying for them.

"Another drink for the master and me, Danny!" Duffy called out again.


Becky pulled up outside the castle. She knew it would soon be dark and she didn't relish the thought of being there on her own. She concluded that she could either sit in the car and wait till Sean came

home (which could be many hours) or pull herself together and go in.

The heavy oak door creaked as she opened it. She fumbled for the light switch and carried Finbar upstairs. After settling him down, she turned on the baby monitor and went down to make herself a coffee and something to eat. She sat down at the table, upset that somehow she had managed to row with Sean again.

A greenish light started to flash on and off under the door to the basement room. As it caught her attention, a shiver went down her spine. She got up and went over to the door. She slowly turned the handle, and as she did the light stopped flashing. The door was locked, and she considered (but quickly dismissed) the idea of getting the key and checking what was happening down there. She hurried upstairs to Finbar, locking the bedroom door behind her.


"Come on, Master - not far now. Lean on me; we'll be home soon," Duffy said, as the pair of them staggered along the road.


Becky came down in the morning, to find Sean and Duffy asleep in armchairs.

"What time did you get in?" Becky said, shaking Sean's shoulder.

He stirred from his sleep. Opening one eye, he said, 'Not too loud, Becks."

It was obvious that he had got very drunk, which was something he normally wouldn't do. But then,

looking over at Duffy, who was snoring, she could see the reason. The only thing she could do was close the door and let them sleep it off.

It was midday when Sean made his appearance in the kitchen, to see Becky was busy cleaning. Unsure what kind of reception he would get, he said sheepishly:

"I don't suppose I'm in your good books?"

Becky gave him the silent treatment.

"Look, I'm sorry, Becks; I don't know what came over me. You know I didn't mean whatever I said that upset you."

"You've just made it worse – that you can't even remember!" she said bitterly. "You've changed so much since we came here; you were never like that towards me. You were always kind and loving. I feel like I don't know you anymore, Sean."

"I'm sorry, Becks. I know I shouldn't let it affect me like it does, but I find myself getting irritable when I can't do what I want to do."

"And what's that?"

"I suppose it's the frustration of living in a castle, and not being able to explore it all."

"You mean the room downstairs?"

"Well, if I'm honest, yes."

"You know why."

"That's what makes it worse. You think there's something down there, and I don't."

"On that subject I'm not willing to compromise, Sean. I've said it before: if this place is coming between us, I want to go home."

"Okay. I promise you I won't be like that again."

"You said that last time."

Still not really knowing what he had done or said yesterday, Sean decided his best chance of making things up with her was to just agree to whatever she said. "I know, but I genuinely mean it." Playing his ace card, he said, "I love you, Becks."

It worked.

"You sure know how to win me over, don't you?" she said.

Sean opened his arms and said, "Come and give me a hug."

"You've got a lot of making up to do. By the way, what time did you get in?"

Knowing that she would have gone to bed and was probably sound asleep when they got back he said, "Not too late. I decided to sleep in the other bedroom so as not to wake you." He thought that was a good answer to keep the peace between them.

"That was considerate of you, Sean; but can you tell me then how it was that I found you asleep in the chair in the big room, along with that drunken fool, Duffy, stinking the place out with drink?"

"Was I? I could have sworn that I was in that bedroom."

"How much did you have to drink?"

"I tried not to, but it was Duffy. He kept ordering them - you know what he's like where drink is involved. And before I knew it, I think I must have had one too many."

"Yeah, yeah," she said, drily. 'So how did it go? Were there many there?"

"Half of Ireland. That reminds me, I have to go back and settle up with Mr Murphy for the drinks."

"What? You have to pay for it all?"

"It appears so; it seems that when there's a wake anyone can go, and the family have to pay. That's what they told me."

"I'll make sure that, when you go, your wake is not around here," she said.

"Thanks, Becks. I love you too."

Duffy walked into the kitchen, "Morning, Missus. Master, do you mind if I makes myself a cuppa?"

"Help yourself; and when you've made it, I want a word with you," Becky said.

Duffy looked at Sean, but all he he did was shrug his shoulders, as if to say 'you're on your own'.

Sitting down with his tea, Duffy said sheepishly, "Yes, Missus?"

"What's the idea of getting my husband drunk? If you want to drink yourself silly, that's your business; but when it involves my husband (and in turn involves me), you cross the line. Do you, hear?"

Duffy grimaced as her loud words went through his head, which was still throbbing from the effects of alcohol. "I hears you, Missus; it won't happen again. You can trust me."

"Too right, it won't. Now, haven't you got work to do, or is that a word you don't understand?" she said, standing over him.

Duffy had been hoping to get a bite to eat, but decided that he he'd better not. He stood up with his mug of tea and left the room.

"I think you were a little hard on him, Becks. I know he doesn't do a lot round here, but sometimes he can be useful, especially outside with all this land," Sean said.

"Why? Do you think he might leave?" she replied.

"He might do. I don't think he has anywhere to go, but he might."

"He's useless anyway, and you can never find him, even if you want to; where he disappears to, I don't know. I hope he does go. And if he doesn't, I'll try my best to be harder on him next time."

"And you say *I've* changed," he said quietly.

"What did you say?"

"Nothing."

"I never did get an answer from you about what Father Dorian said. So what did he think - about exorcism?" Becky asked.

"He said he would ring us."

"Didn't you tell him I was concerned and I wanted it done?"

"Of course I did; he said he would try and get here next week."

"Try! Didn't you tell him it was urgent?" she said, raising her voice.

With a sigh, Sean said, "Yes, but you must remember – this is Ire . . ."

"Don't keep saying that!" she interrupted. "I'm waiting to get it bricked up. He'd better come this week, or else."

Knowing what her 'or else' meant, Sean replied, "He will." Changing the subject, he said, "How's Finbar?"

"Well, if you were here, instead of getting drunk with that old fool, you would know," she said.

"Becks, I thought we made it up?"

"We did. I mean - we have. Sorry, Honey, it's just there's something about that Duffy that makes my blood boil, and he's creepy. I swear I can hear him at night walking around. It's one more reason I keep the

bedroom door locked. Anyway, Finbar's asleep; he's due to wake up for another feed. Why don't you go and get him, while I finish cleaning?"

"Sure."


Becky could hear the phone ringing in the hall. She was expecting Sean to answer it, but it kept on ringing.

She shouted out: "Honey, can you get that? I'm changing Finbar!" But there was no answer from him. As the phone kept on ringing, she assumed it was important and took Finbar as he was and rushed to the phone.

"Yes! Becky Finnegan speaking," she said, realising she must have sounded abrupt and annoyed.

"Hello Becky, Father Dorian here; your husband asked me to call, to make arrangements to visit your place."

"Hi, Father Dorian. Oh, please excuse me for answering like that. I must have sounded terribly rude. I thought Sean was getting it and I was right in the middle of seeing to the baby."

"I've had worse from people. Now, I can come about three this afternoon - if that's convenient?"

"Yes, that would be fine. I'm not going anywhere. Thank you so much, Father Dorian," she said with relief.

"Don't thank me yet. I don't know what we'll find - if anything," he replied. "Till this afternoon then."

"Were you calling me?" Sean said, coming out of the library.

"Yes I was. Didn't you hear the phone ringing?"

"No . . ."

But Sean did hear it. He'd suspected it was Father Dorian phoning to make arrangements about the exorcism, and he'd hoped that, by not answering it, it would give him a little more time to go down into the basement room.

"I don't know how you didn't hear it. It's not as if the library is at the top of the building."

"This old place has solid doors and thick walls, Becks. Anyway who was it?"

"Father Dorian - phoning about coming here."

"So when is he coming?" Sean asked.

"This afternoon. Isn't that good news?"

"I wish you'd checked with me first! I was going to surprise you and take you and Finbar out this afternoon. Can you not phone him back and tell him it's not convenient?"

"Since we've been here, you have never taken us out; and now, the day Father Dorian wants to come, you decide that you want to! No Sean, he's coming; you know my feelings on the subject. You can take us out tomorrow."

Sean knew he was defeated. He didn't want to antagonise her any further so he said, "Okay. Tomorrow it is."


At 3 o'clock on the dot the front door bell rang. Duffy, who had come in for his afternoon mug of tea, went to open the door.

"It's you, Father Dorian. I didn't know you were coming. Have you come to see the master?"

Father Dorian didn't answer the question, but said, "Duffy, I haven't seen you at mass or confession, and I suspect you have a lot to confess - don't you?"

Duffy just stood there stuck for words; he had been dreading this. For ages now he had been avoiding Father Dorian, for just such a reason.

"Just as I suspected! You haven't an answer. So, are you going to make it worse and keep me standing here, or are you going to let me in to see Mr Finnegan?"

"You'd better follow me then, Father," was all he could muster.

Taking him down to the kitchen, Duffy said, "If you wait here, I'll go and fetch the master."

"Master, Father Dorian's here to see you," he called to the upper room.

Becky heard the name and came down, "Where is he, Duffy?"

"I put him down in the kitchen; is that all right?"

"Yes, Duffy," she said, hurrying past him.

"Father Dorian, thank you for coming. Did Duffy make you a drink?"

"No, but as I have to get back for evening mass, I'd like to get this over with; so I won't have one, thank you. So where is this room?"

"There," she said pointing to the door.

Father Dorian walked over and turned the knob. "It's locked!"

"Oh sorry, Father. I keep it locked; to be honest, it's to keep Sean from going down there. I won't be long - I keep the key hidden upstairs (so he can't find it)."

Duffy, who was listening outside the door, realised the master would be in trouble. He knew the key she

156

was going to fetch didn't fit, as it was the one he and Sean had swapped previously when she had demanded that they gave her the key. If she tried to unlock the door, the game was up for the pair of them. He quickly set off to find Sean to warn him.

"Sorry about that, Father Dorian," Becky said, returning with the key. She put it in the lock and tried to turn it.

"I don't understand why it won't open!"

Sean came rushing in, with Duffy close behind, hoping to get downstairs before Becky got back. He realised he had no choice but to open the door, even though it meant that Father Dorian would have access to the room for the exorcism. He knew that, once he had done it, Becky would have the door bricked up; but worse still, she would know that he had deceived her yet again.

But it was too late. As soon as he appeared, Becky said:

"Sean, can you tell me why the key you gave me doesn't fit this door?"

Turning to Duffy, he said, "I *told* you to make sure you got the right key from your box! Now, go and get it!"

Duffy didn't know what he was supposed to do, as he knew Sean had the key on him.

"It will be quicker, Master, if you could help me find it. You know what I'm like; my old memory isn't as good as it used to be."

Sean had been going to suggest that, but it sounded more convincing coming from Duffy. Becky sighed. She didn't want to make a scene in front of Father Dorian, so she just said, "Make sure you hurry! Father Dorian hasn't got long."

The pair of them left the room - Sean behind, pushing Duffy up the stairs to make him hurry. At the top of the stairs he said to Duffy, "Here, take the key and get back down there. I'll be down in a minute."

"Here you are, Missus. It's the right key," Duffy said, handing it to her.

Becky snatched it from his hand and unlocked the door. "There you are, Father - it's all yours," she said, stepping to one side.

Father Dorian opened the door. "Mother of God! What's that stench down there?"

# Chapter 10

"That's a stench from hell, Father! I smelt it before when I was down there," Duffy replied.

Father Dorian grimaced and asked, "Is there a light down there?"

"Aye, Father, it was my fair self that put it there. Here, let me turn it on for you."

Father Dorian, taking out his cross, went slowly down the steps.

"Those steps are slippery, Father. You might want to take care," Duffy called down to him. "Do you want me to close the door?"

"No And no more talking! I'm trying to listen," he replied.

"I was only trying to be helpful, Missus," Duffy said as he turned to Becky.

"Best you leave it to someone who knows what they're doing, and wait in case he wants you to give him a hand," Becky replied.

The words 'give him a hand' caused alarm bells, as he couldn't think of anything worse then going

down there, especially with the priest. Although he would be carrying out an exorcism of the room, Duffy knew that he would be at risk of it being performed on *him*.

"I have just remembered, Missus, I've a fence to repair before it gets dark. I'd better get going."

Before Becky had a chance to speak, he left the room. She stood at the top of the stairs, listening to Father Dorian reciting prayers. Then she heard him starting to make his way up the steps.

"Well, Father was there anything down there?"

"Apart from that foul stench, nothing manifested itself; but, if there *was* something down there, I'm sure with the prayers it's gone now. But I would say, it has an awful atmosphere."

"With what's gone on down there, I should think there must be," Becky replied.

"Some evil events must have taken place over the centuries. That can cause the atmosphere. I would lock the door and throw away the key."

"Yes, I will do that, but also I'm having it bricked up," she replied.

"Very sensible. Well, I have to get going. Let me know if there are any more problems; but I think you'll be okay now. Might we see you in church on Sunday? I was going to say: 'with that heathen Duffy' but that would be asking for a miracle," he chuckled.

"As I said at the funeral service, I am a believer – but I'm not Catholic."

"Well the doors are open to you, if you should change your mind. I'll say goodbye then."

Becky followed him over to the stairs.

"Don't worry about seeing me out. I can find my own way; you stay here with the baby."

160

"Well, if you're sure. Goodbye, Father, and thank you."

Sean watched from the window as the priest left, then went down to Becky.

"He's gone then; how did it go?" he enquired.

"How did you think it would go? And if you had been here instead of hiding, you would have heard what he said," she replied crossly.

"Are you upset with me again?"

"What do you expect, Sean - trying to fob me off with the wrong key? Well, I have the key now and the door is locked. That's how it's going to stay and you're not getting your hands on it. And you can tell that to that fool of a friend of yours too!"

"That's fine, Becks, whatever you say; and, by the way, he's not my friend. So did he hear or see anything down there?"

"No, but he's confident that we won't have any more problems."

"Good, then we can use the room, maybe for a wine cellar or something?" he said.

Beck didn't answer. The only plan she had for the room was to have it bricked up and she already had the builder on standby for tomorrow. But, for that to happen, she needed Sean and Duffy away from the place, so they couldn't interfere.

"I haven't said anything, but I've been looking online for a little car, and I've found one in Cork. I was wondering if you would take Duffy with you and go and look at it for me. And if it's any good bring it back."

Becky wasn't lying; she had been looking and had found one that she liked. She wasn't really in a hurry for it, but it was a good excuse to get rid of them both.

"You should have said you wanted a car. I would have got you one when we came here. Why don't you come with me? It would save taking Duffy, and I did say I wanted to take you out. We could go and see the car and then stop off on the way back somewhere. Anyway, I don't know if Duffy has a licence or if he can even drive."

"No, it means taking Finbar with us, and trying to look at a car with a screaming baby is no good. You go with Duffy; I'm sure he can drive. He did tell us that he drove a tractor and, anyway, even if he hasn't got a licence and got stopped, I'm sure he'd talk his way out of it."

"Well, I rather go with you, Becks, but if you're sure?"

"I'm sure. If you leave early, you can be back before it gets dark."

"I'll go and tell Duffy."

While Sean was out of the room she made the call to the builder. Fortunately, the bribe of extra money made him willing to come at very short notice.


"Well, there you are - a fine job, if I say so myself! Would you not agree, Mrs Finnegan?"

"Yes, that's fine. There's one more thing while you're here. Would you move that big dresser in front of the doorway, then I'll pay you," she said.

"That would cover up my fine work. I thought you said you were pleased with it?" he replied, taken aback by her request.

"There's nothing wrong with your work, Mr O'Sullivan. I just want the dresser moved there."

Wanting to get paid, and knowing it wouldn't happen until the dresser was moved, he said no more and went over to the dresser. With a lot of puffing and stopping, he finally got it where she wanted it.

"There you are. Would you be seeing your way to paying me a bit more for my sweat and my time?"

"That would be a 'no'; I'm paying you over the top now. Here's what we agreed. Good bye, Mr O'Sullivan."

Grumbling to himself, he managed a 'good-bye' and left.


"We're back, Becks!" Sean called out, as he closed the door behind him.

"I'm upstairs with Finbar," Becky called down. "Is Duffy with you?"

"Yes."

"Get him to put the kettle on. I'll be down in a minute."

The first thing Sean noticed as he went into the kitchen was that the pile of bricks had gone and that the dresser was in front of the doorway.

"Duffy, did you know my wife was doing this today?" he asked.

"No, Master, I didn't, honestly."

Just as he was saying that, Becky walked into the room.

"How's that for getting something done around here?" she said, with smug smile.

"Is this the reason you sent us off for the day?" Sean asked.

163

"I would have to answer truthfully (unlike other people in this place) and say: yes," she replied.

She could tell by the look on Sean's face that he wasn't happy about it.

"Honey, it was that or leave. Knowing how you like it here, I've kind of done you a favour. You get to stay and I get to stop worrying. I'd say that was a win-win situation, wouldn't you agree?"

"That sounds good to me, Master. That would be a good plan, that it would," Duffy said, to fill the silence.

Sean looked daggers at him.

"Yes, I'm okay with that Becks, although a little disappointed that I didn't get a chance to see what it was like down there. Still, the main thing is, as you said, you won't be worrying anymore. Well, you haven't asked!"

"Asked what?" she replied.

"About the car! Or were you so caught up with having the door bricked up you forgot all about it?"

"Oh, yes the car. Was it any good?"

"You can see for yourself - it's outside," Sean replied.

"Duffy, while you're drinking your tea, if you hear Finbar cry on the monitor, come out and tell me," she said, rushing up the stairs to go outside. Sean followed her.

"Well, what do you think? Duffy says it drives well."

Becky opened the door. "Did you stop off at the pub?"

"How did you know that?"

"It stinks of Duffy's drinking."

"It was only for the one; you know I won't drink and drive."

"I know *you* would only have one, but the day Duffy does . . . " she trailed off, unable to think of a catastrophe big enough. "But thanks, Honey, I really didn't expect you to bring it back."

"The good thing though, it had a bit of road tax on it, so it was just a case of a telephone call to the insurance company."

"Missus, the young master is awake!" called Duffy, out of breath as he came up the stairs.

"You go, Becks, and I'll lock it up," Sean said to her.

"Leave the door open for a while, Honey, and let the stink out of there."

Duffy heard what Becky said.

"What stink is that, Master?"

"My wife says you've stunk the car out with drink, Duffy."

Duffy stuck his head in the car. "I smells no stink in here, Master!"

"Never mind, Duffy. Now, did you know anything about my wife having that door bricked up?"

"All I knows, Master, is that she asked me the other day if I has a brother who's a builder. I tells the Missus: no, but I do have one that's a postman, a good postman too, that he is. And I do have a cousin, Pat, who might be something like a builder; but seeing how good those bricks have been laid, it wouldn't be his work. That's all I knows. Would it be that you are not too happy about it being done, Master?"

"No Duffy, I'm not. (But that's between you and me. Do you understand?)"

"I understands, that I do, Master. I knows about being unhappy. Did I tell you about the time when I was a lad, when everybody forgot my birthday?"

"No, but not now, Duffy." Sean knew he would be going on for hours if he let him start.

Disappointed, Duffy said, "I might get unhappy, Master, but there's no need for you to be. I can tell you something that will make you happy, if you want to hear it?"

"What are you muttering about, Duffy?"

"I said I knows something that will make you happy."

"And what would that be, Duffy?"

"I knows another way to get into that room."

"Unless you didn't notice, to get into that room you'd have to walk through a brick wall. Can you do that, Duffy?"

Duffy went into one of his thinking modes, then said, "If it's anything like the last time I walked into a wall, my nose took a banging, that it did. If it's alright with you, Master, I don't think I want to try."

Sean just shook his head. He could see why Becky called him an old fool.

"Come on, Duffy. Let's go indoors."

"Don't you want me to show you then, Master?"
Humouring him, Sean said, "Yes, okay - show me then."

Duffy turned and started to walk up the drive, away from the castle. "This way, Master."

Sean, called out to Becky, "I won't be long. Duffy wants to show me something."

"Okay - as long as you're not; I need you to help me with one of the boxes," she called back.

"So where are we going, Duffy?"

"Over here, Master," Duffy said, taking him towards the big stone.

"Duffy, it's just a big stone. What's that got to do with getting into the room?"

"No, not the stone, Master. It's behind them bushes; come - I'll show you."
Duffy parted the bushes and held them back for Sean to get through.

"There are only more stones here. What am I supposed to be looking for?"

Duffy started to unstack several stones, revealing a small entrance just big enough to squeeze through.

"I used to play here as a lad. The entrance was small then, but over the years I made it big enough so as I could get in there. Do you want to go in there, Master?"

"Are you saying this leads all the way to the room?"

"Yes. At the end there's a big stone that divides the tunnel from the room."

"So how do you get into that room?" Sean asked.

"Why don't you go in and I'll show you?"

"It looks pretty dark in there; how do we see where we are going?"

"I 'as a torch - just inside; follow me, Master."
As Sean went inside he could see that he was standing in a high, vaulted tunnel.

"Who else knows of this?" he said, amazed at the size of it.

"No one living; it's my secret place."

"So, is this where you go when we can't find you?"

"I don't as much as I used to, Master, but I likes to have a place that I can come to and think. It's my home."

"Duffy, how can you call a cave your home?"

"Because it's mine. I found it and it's mine!" he said with an aggressive, strange tone to his voice.

"Okay, Duffy; if you say it's yours - it's yours. So, if this is your secret place and it's so special to you, why did you show it to me?"

"Oh, I thinks it will stay a secret, Master, that I do," Duffy said with a wry grin.

Sean made his way along the tunnel with Duffy behind him.

"So this is the big stone?" Sean said, taking hold of one of the iron rings. "How does it open?"

"It's a clever stone - watch." Duffy went to the side of the stone and pushed on a smaller protruding stone; as he did the small stone moved into the rock.

"Pull on one of those rings, Master."

Sean gripped one of the rings with both hands and the big stone pivoted from the middle and swung open, to reveal a huge, dark cavern.

Sean grabbed the torch out of Duffy's hand and said, "Is *this* the same place as the steps from the kitchen lead to?"

"Yes, Master. Now you can go in and be happy."

"Now that I know how to get here, I'll leave exploring it till another day. I told my wife I wouldn't be long."

"I'll tell you what, Master, I'll go back and tell the Missus you won't be too much longer. It would be a shame to spoil a chance of being happy, that it would."

"Whatever you do, Duffy, don't you tell her where I am!"

"Oh, rest assured, Master, I won't be doing that. It's a secret, that it is," he said, walking away.

His chuckling could be heard along the tunnel.

Sean made his way into the room and the big stone swung shut behind him.

# Chapter 11

Becky looked at the clock; it had been over an hour since Sean had said he wouldn't be long. Although the signal at the castle was extremely poor, she tried repeatedly to ring Sean's mobile, but the call failed each time.  So having no choice, she took Finbar with her to look outside for him. She knew that he'd gone off with Duffy, who'd apparently wanted to show him something, but where she didn't know.

"If that Duffy has taken him down the pub!" she said to Finbar. "Sean! Duffy!" she shouted out.

Duffy appeared from the woodshed. "You wanted me, Missus?"

"Where's my husband?"

"I haven't got him, Missus."

"I know you haven't got him.  I'm asking where he is?  He went off with you, didn't he?"

"Did he?"

"Yes, Duffy.  He said that you wanted to show him something; and that was over an hour ago."

Duffy knew he couldn't tell her where Sean was, as he would be in trouble again - with both of them.

"I showed him the view from the edge of the grounds, that looks out to the sea. He said he liked the view and was happy to stay there a while, so I left him there and came back - as I had my chores to do."

Becky knew she could do nothing but wait for Sean to come back, as she knew how far the place was, and it was too far to walk there with Finbar.

"Missus, if you like, I'll look after the young master while you go and look for him."

Becky couldn't help noticing the weird grin on his face as he said it, which made her feel uncomfortable.

"No, Duffy, you go and find him and ask him if he could come home now."

"No problem, Missus," he said and went back into the woodshed.

Thinking he went in there to get something, Becky waited until she realised that he wasn't coming out.

"*Duffy!*" she shouted.

"Yes, Missus?"

"I want you to go *now*!"

"Oh, right. Yes, I'll go now, Missus."

"Good, and what have you got to tell him?"

Duffy stood there with his usual vacant look.

Exasperated, she said, "Oh, for goodness sake, you old fool! Go and tell him he's to come home now."

Duffy grumbled, and walked off muttering, "Old fool? I'll show you who's the fool."


Sean's curiosity about the room was quashed when he saw that there was nothing but four damp,

stone walls and some markings scratched into them. He turned to the stone door to leave, thinking that all he had to do was push it. When he found it didn't open, panic went through him. In desperation, he put his shoulder to it, but the stone still didn't move. To add to his fear, the torch beam started to dim, which told him that the batteries were running out of power. It would only be a matter of time before the room would be engulfed in darkness.

He didn't know when Duffy would be back, if at all. He knew how forgetful he was, especially if he had been drinking. To make it worse, nobody knew he was there. As much as he didn't want to, he knew that his only hope was to ring his wife. With the little light that remained, he dialled Becky. The phone rang then went dead.

He realised that he had no signal, especially being underground and surrounded by solid stone. He thought about banging on the door at the top of the stairs, but as it was bricked up and with the big dresser in front of it, he knew that the chance of Becky hearing it was zero.

In the dimness, he noticed the electric light on the wall in the corner, which Duffy said he had fixed up for his grandfather. He could just about see the switch at the top of the stairs, so made his way up to it and flicked the switch to 'on'. The room lit up, then went dark, then to his relief, it came back on. It continued to flicker off and on, which was at least better than no light at all. Thinking the problem was the switch, he tried switching it off and on.

The grinding of the stone door opening made him start to turn around.

"At last, Duffy! I thought you'd forgotten I was here!"

But it was not Duffy standing there. To Sean's horror, looking at him in the flashing light was the grotesque figure of a one-eyed man. His hammering on the oak door was to no avail, as the man, with a white-hot blade, made his way up the stairs.

Minutes later, the only sounds in the room were the intermittent ring of Sean's phone on the ground, and the sound of steel scraping into the rock.


Becky went back inside. She thought she'd try again to ring Sean. As it connected she could hear the muffled ring of his phone, then the signal died. She was convinced that it had come from somewhere in the kitchen, but couldn't see how that was possible as there was no sign of the phone. She tried again, but her phone said: 'No Service'.

She looked at her watch again, to see that two hours had now passed and, because it was getting dark, she couldn't help thinking that something was wrong. Seeing that Finbar was asleep, she rushed upstairs and stood in the entrance to see if there was any sign of Duffy coming back with Sean.

There was nothing to see or hear, apart from the birds getting ready for the night. "Where are you, Sean? Please come back," she said softly. She didn't know what to do, as she was on her own with the baby, unable to do anything but wait. She went back to the kitchen and began pacing up and down, occasionally looking out of the window, hoping to see something.

Hearing the main door close, she rushed upstairs, to see Duffy standing there alone.

"I couldn't see him, Missus; he wasn't there," Duffy said.

"What do mean, *he wasn't there*? Where is he then?"

"I don't know, Missus; he's gone, gone an' disappeared, that he has."

"Do you know Mr Murphy's phone number?"

"Why would you be wanting his number, Missus?"

"As much as I wouldn't want him to be there, he just might be."

"No, Missus. What would I be wanting to know his number for? I'll tell you what, as tired as I am from a hard day's work, I'll go there to see if the master's there.'

"Thank you, Duffy. There's one other thing: don't you dare have a drink, do you hear? I want you back here, to tell me if he's not there. And if he is, you bring him back! Do you understand?"

"Don't worry about that, Missus; if he's there I'll bring him back, that I will."

Duffy went back to the tunnel and made his way to the big stone door. Opening it, he said, "Master, I think it's time you came back! The missus is blaming me."

The light was flashing on and off but Duffy could see, to his horror, the master lying on his back, dead and with his eyes removed. He was overcome with panic as he tried to decide what to do. He knew that if he went back and told Becky the master was dead (and especially where), his life at the castle would be over. He also knew that this time he would be the prime suspect with the Garda.

He reasoned that, as no one else knew the master was in the room (or about the tunnel), the chances of anyone ever finding the body were remote. So he decided to keep quiet. He turned the light off, closed the stone door, then made his way out of the tunnel and headed to the bar.


It had been two hours since Duffy left for Murphy's. Becky knew she should have realised that giving Duffy an excuse to go to the pub was a mistake, and that she wouldn't see him till morning. She didn't really think Sean would have gone to the bar alone, but she rang directory enquiries and got the number, so she could make sure. She dialled the bar, but it rang and rang endlessly. Either it was out of order or no one was bothering to answer. She tried repeatedly – with the same result, getting more and more frustrated. She was at her wit's end, not knowing whom to turn to, as she hadn't made any friends since moving there.

It had been four hours since Sean had disappeared.

"Lord, what am I going to do?" Maybe it was because she was desperate, but they were the only words she could say.

The word 'Pray!' came to her. Even though she had had a Christian upbringing and was taught in times of crisis to pray, it was the last thing that she had thought of.

"Lord, I need your help. Sorry for not turning to you before, but I don't know what to do. I'm in this place, not knowing whom to call that can help me. I

know Sean doesn't believe in you, but please bring him home."

Then Maggie's words came to her: "*If you ever need me.*"

"What did I do with her number?" she said aloud. She started searching the pockets of her jacket, which revealed nothing. Then she rememberd the coat she had on at the funeral service. Quickly she went upstairs to her room and took it out of the wardrobe. To her relief, she found the number. Even though it was late she decided to ring her.

"Is that Maggie? Sorry to ring so late. It's Becky Finnegan - we met at the church."

"Ah yes, my dear. You sound a bit upset; what's wrong?"

"Oh, Maggie, Sean's disappeared. I'm here on my own and don't know where to turn!"

"What do you mean, dear, 'disappeared'?"

"He said he was going with Duffy to see something and that he wouldn't be long. That was over four hours ago. I have this dreadful feeling something's happened to him."

"Have you seen Duffy?"

"Yes, he says he left him at the viewpoint that looks out to sea. But when I sent Duffy to find him, he said he's not there. What do I do, Maggie?"

"Look, sit tight and try not to worry. I'll pop next door to my young friend, Doreen, and ask if she can give me a lift. I'm sure she will, so I should be with you in about twenty minutes. Now, I'm sure everything is going to be okay; I'll see you soon, my dear."

Becky tried ringing Murphy's again but there was still no answer, then she moved upstairs to one of the front rooms so she could watch out for the car lights coming down the drive. As soon as they appeared she hurried to the front door to meet Maggie.

"Thank you, thank you for coming!" Becky said, hugging her.

"You're welcome, my dear. This is my friend, Doreen," Maggie replied kindly. Seeing the state Becky was in, she said, "Come on, my dear - let's make you a nice cup of tea. It will make you feel better, you'll see. Doreen, you go on home, dear, I'll stay here - Becky shouldn't be alone and I know you need to get back."

"Thank you, Doreen," Becky said, as she left.

"Now, you come with me," Maggie said, taking her by the hand to the kitchen.

Maggie sat her down and put the kettle on. Having made the tea, she sat down with Becky and said, "Now, let's start at the beginning."

Becky repeated what she had told her over the phone.

"So Duffy hasn't come back? Well, that's no surprise - the useless, good-for-nothing . . ." Maggie ranted. "Have you tried ringing the bar yourself?"

"Yes – it seems like about fifty times, but no one ever answers." She tried again and held the phone near Maggie so she could hear the endless ringing.

"Either it's out of order, or there's so much noise in there that they can't hear it – drunken lot!"

"Do you think I should report Sean missing, Maggie?"

"I know it's worrying, my dear, but why don't you give it till morning, in case he *is* at Murphy's bar," Maggie replied.

"Oh, I wish that Duffy would come back - at least I would know!"

"That useless lump!" Maggie sighed.

"Thank you for staying with me, Maggie. I don't know what I would have done."

"Now, let's get you upstairs."

"What about you?" Becky asked.

"Don't worry about me, dear. I know this place well; I'll sleep in one of the spare rooms."


"Morning, my dear. I've made you a nice cup of tea. I won't ask if you had a good night, as I heard you pacing up and down. It's the reason I didn't wake you early."

"Why, what time is it?"

"Gone ten, my dear."

"Has he come back?"

"No, my dear; nor has Duffy. But then, I didn't expect him to, knowing where he went. Look, you drink your tea and I'll take the young master down and feed him, then I'll cook us some breakfast."

"I don't think I can eat, Maggie."

"Well, you come down when you're ready, and we'll discuss what we're going to do," Maggie replied.


Becky made her way into the kitchen, to see Finbar being spoilt by Maggie.

"Right, my dear. I've phoned Doreen and told her that Sean didn't come back last night. I asked her if

she would get her husband, Tommy, who's the local Garda, to drop by. So, as hard as it is, my dear, we can only wait. Would you reconsider have a little bite to eat?"

"It's the not knowing that's hard, Maggie. Oh, why doesn't that Duffy come back? At least I would know something."

"I know, my dear, I know," Maggie said, putting her arm around her.


The bang on the front door made them jump. Maggie said, "That will be Tommy. I'll go, my dear."

"Hello, Maggie. Doreen said you'd be here. Has he come back yet?" Tommy asked.

"No. You'd better come in; she's in a bit of a state. This is Tommy, my dear - Doreen's husband."

"Hello, Mrs Finnegan; would you be up to answering a few questions?"

"Yes, whatever I can tell you - if it helps to find him," Becky replied.

"When was the last time you saw him?"

"Yesterday afternoon, about 4 o'clock; we were out the front - he was showing me the car he had bought me. I left him outside because Finbar was awake."

"Finbar?" he asked.

"Yes, my son over there. Duffy was told to come and get me if he woke up."

"Duffy, you say? Does he still work here?"

"Yes. You sound surprised, officer."

"A bit - after the last two times."

"What do you mean: 'last two times'?" she asked, puzzled.

Seeing the look on Becky's face, Maggie said, "I think Tommy here means that there was a little suspicion towards him about the deaths of the last two Mr Finnegans. (But he hasn't got a brain to do anything like that.)"

"You don't think that he's responsible do you?"

"I think we're getting ahead of ourselves here, Mrs Finnegan. You were saying you left your husband outside."

Becky repeated the whole story of what had happened the day before.

"The only place that I could think of him going was Mr Murphy's bar. So, as much as I didn't want to, I sent Duffy there to see, but he hasn't come back yet."

"I told her that's the worst thing you could ask that good-for-nothing, useless, old fool - to go to a bar. I told her: you won't see him until lunchtime at least," Maggie added.

"Thank you, Maggie, I'll take it from here. Have you tried ringing the bar?"

"I've lost count of the times I've tried, including this morning. There's never an answer."

"It might be out of order. Does your husband drink a lot, Mrs Finnegan?" he asked.

"No! Not at all; well apart from an occasional night out with his friends back home, but since we've been here he hasn't really. The last time was at his father's wake, about a month ago."

So tell me, Mrs Finnegan, how were things between you? Have you been rowing at all?"

"No! We don't row anymore than any other couple. What are you trying to say?"

"I'm just trying to get an idea of his state of mind yesterday. Had he been upset about anything?"

Becky paused, then said, "The only thing he looked a bit upset about (well, maybe I should say more like *disappointed*) was that I had the doorway to the cellar room bricked up while he was out yesterday. He had his heart set on investigating it and, as his grandfather and father died down there, I didn't want him going anywhere near it."

"So, did you argue about it?" he asked her.

"No! I told you we don't argue," she said, bursting into tears.

"Tommy Deneen! You're about as sensitive as a cow's backside. Your father wouldn't have put it like that; it was a loss to the force when he retired," Maggie chided.

"I'm only doing my job - the way I know how, Maggie. Look, I think I've got enough. I'll call into Murphy's on my way to the station; he's probably there, having had one too many."

"If you see that Duffy . . ."

"Don't worry, Mrs Finnegan; I'll be having a word with him. Meanwhile, if he does come back, let me know."

"I'll see him out my dear," Maggie said, getting up from the chair.


"Good morning to you, Tommy; are you here for a drink or on business?"

"You know I never drink while I'm on duty, Danny. Sean Finnegan's wife (from up at the castle) has reported him missing; well, put it this way: he didn't come home last night. Would you happen to have seen him?"

"No. The last time he was in here was about a month ago, at his daddy's wake."

"What about . . . don't worry - I can see him," Tommy said, as he looked around the room.

As he walked towards Duffy, Danny said, "If it's Duffy you're after, you won't get much out of him. He had a heavy session yesterday; he's been here all night."

Tommy asked if Duffy had come alone.

"Aye, he did that. He looked quite flustered, and I asked him what he'd been up to. He said that they were blaming him for 'losing the master'. When I asked him what he meant, he just rambled on, saying that it wasn't his fault. I gave him his pint and he sat at his table, drinking one after the other. As I said, with the amount of drink inside him - I don't think you will get much out of him."

In spite of Danny's words, Tommy shook Duffy by the shoulder. "Duffy! Duffy, you drunkard, wake up!" he demanded.

Duffy stirred and mumbled, "It's not my fault, Missus."

"What did he say, Danny?"

"Something about 'the Missus'."

"He's not married is he?" Tommy asked.

"No. No woman in their right mind would marry him," Danny chuckled. "No, I think he calls Mrs Finnegan 'the Missus'. Here, put this under his nose - it's never failed yet," he said, giving Tommy a pint of ale.

"What's so special about this then?"

"It's his favourite beer - 'Black Diamond'; he drinks nothing else."

Duffy's nose twitched.  One eye opened, then the other.

"Lunch, Duffy!" Danny called to him.

Instantly Duffy sat up and took a mouthful. Recognising the person looking at him, he gave a loud belch and said, "Your's isn't a face I want to wake up to, Tommy Deneen.  What do you want with me? I've not done anything wrong."

"Just a few questions, Duffy; then I'll let you drown in your drink," Tommy said.

"Danny, it's a poor day when I can't have a drink in peace anymore," Duffy complained.

Danny carried on wiping the glasses, pretending not to hear him.

"What's happened to Sean Finnegan, Duffy?"

"Don't know what you mean."

"According to Mrs Finnegan, you took him to the viewpoint and he hasn't come back."

"Did I?"

"Well, you told her you did; or is that not true and you took him somewhere else?"

Duffy just sat there looking vacant, then let out another belch.  Unfortunately for Tommy, his face caught the full blast of stale alcohol, making him grimace in disgust.

"Better out than in," Duffy said.  "Ah yes, I remember now; yes, the viewpoint, to be sure - that's where I took him."

"Why did you take him there?" Tommy asked.

"Because he was unhappy about the Missus bricking up that door so he couldn't see the room.  So I, being a good, loyal Duffy, thought he would be happy if I showed him the view. It's a nice place to go

when you're unhappy. I've spent many a time up there. There was a particular time when . . . "

"So, did you leave him there?" Tommy interrupted, not wanting to hear one of his stories.

"That I did, Sir, then I went back to my woodshed as I had work to do. So, has he not come back?" he asked, innocently.

"No. That's why I'm here, you being the last person to see him. If you remember anything more, you come and tell me; do you hear?"

"I won't be doing that because I told you all I know. But I reckons he's gone the way of his daddy."

"What do you mean by that, Duffy?"

Tapping the side of his nose, Duffy said, "Like daddy - like son. He's run off and left them. That's what I reckons."

"How do know that about his daddy?" Tommy asked.

"I'm repeating what the master told me. It was right here, to be sure, when I first met them. He told me that his daddy left without a word when he was a boy, and that he hadn't heard of him since. That was his exact words, I think. Danny, can I have another one here?"

Tommy made a note in his book. "Oh, by the way, when you've finished that, you'd better get back to the castle; Mrs Finnegan's waiting for you, and there's an old friend of yours there too," he called out to him, as he made his way to the door. "Hey Danny, I'll be in for that pint on my way home."

"It will be here waiting for you when you're ready," Danny replied.

"Friend? I've got no friends . . . well, maybe Angus, but he's never been to the castle. Who's the friend then?" Duffy called out.

"Maggie!" Tommy called back, "And God help you!"

"Mother of God! Not Maggie! She's no friend of mine. I thought I saw the last of that old crow when she left the castle. Danny, give me a large glass of the poteen from under the bar - I'm going to need it."

# Chapter 12

"Maggie, I don't know how, but I can't help thinking that room has something to do with Sean's disappearance."

"But it's blocked up, my dear; how can that be possible?" Maggie answered.

"I know. I can't explain it; it's just an overwhelming feeling. Did I mention that I have an old book that was found down there?"

"No . . . so have you been in that room then?"

"No; I found it hidden behind some others on the top shelf in the library. I'm sure Duffy hid it there. (He'd told me previously that when he found Sean's grandfather down there, there was a book open on his lap.)"

"How do you know it's the same book?"

"Because he mentioned that it had the name 'Balor' on it and a carving on the cover of an eye. Would you like to see it? I have it hidden upstairs."

"Well . . . yes, but I can't see any connection with the room and Sean's disappearance."

"Maybe not Maggie, but the book might just reveal something. Look, I'll only be a minute."

Becky came rushing back down with the book and sat down next to Maggie.

"That's an ugly looking book cover, if ever I saw one," Maggie said, handling the book.

"Yes, it is, and there are some weird symbols and writings inside," Becky said, opening it.

"Mary and Joseph! What's that smell?" Maggie said, as she reared back from it.

"Sorry, Maggie. I forgot to mention it; yes, that's what hit me when I first opened it. I've never smelt anything like it before."

"I've smelt that before. Give me a minute . . . Yes! I remember. It was when Mr Finnegan Senior was down in that room with Duffy. I went over to the door and looked down the steps. That's where I've smelt it before; I remember saying, 'It stinks down there like rotten meat! You got a body down there, Duffy?' And I don't think I'm far wrong about the smell."

"You know, Maggie, I'm sure that whenever Duffy comes into the room, I can smell that same smell."

"Oh, my dear, that's Duffy's natural smell. Between you and me, I don't think he bathes from one year to another," she chuckled, wrinkling her nose.

Becky turned the page, "See, this writing - can you understand it?"

"No, but I have an old friend who might: 'Professor David Trant'. I'm sure he's retired now. Hark at me, my dear! He's the same age as me; he must be," she chuckled. "You don't realise how the years go by. Make the best of your life, dear; it has a nasty habit of flying by and, before you know what's happened, you're old. Sorry, I'm rambling on again. I'm afraid

that's another part of getting old. Anyway, I know his field was something like: Irish History and Folklore, at Cork University; he's got all those letters after his name. I'm sure he would love to see this book."

"Does he live nearby?" Becky asked.

"Yes, not too far. You know, dear, I hadn't seen him for ages. Then I bumped into him in the town about three weeks ago. Let me ring Doreen, to see if she would take us to see him."

"There's no need - we can take one of the cars outside; I can drive. But will he be in?" Becky said.

"I'm sure he will. He was being pushed around in a wheelchair, and, if he wanted to go out, he was telling me, he had to rely on family or helpers. So when do you want to go?"

"Now," Becky said, enthusiastically.


"This is his place; nice isn't it?" Maggie said.

Becky pulled into the drive of a stone-built bungalow overlooking a meadow.

"It sure is a nice place to retire to; it's so peaceful."

"I must warn you, my dear - he's a bit of an old charmer, but he's harmless."

Maggie went on ahead, while Becky got Finbar out of the car.


David saw the car pull up from his window and hobbled with his stick to the door.

"Well, if it isn't the Love of my Life! I knew you couldn't stay away from me too long."

"Away with you! You're too old for that kind of talk," Maggie laughed.

"And who is this lovely young cailín you've brought to see me?" he said, adjusting his bow tie.

"This is my friend, Becky, and Master Finbar."

"Hello," he said with a friendly smile.

"She's married! So you can put any of your ideas out of your head," Maggie said, putting him in his place.

Becky could see that David wasn't like the professors she had met back on the campus where she had worked. But he *was* what she imagined a professor would look like. Standing there in his corduroy trousers with cardigan and bow tie, he had a certain charm. Although he was old now, his handsome looks were still apparent.

"Hi, Professor Trant," she said.

"Please, call me David. 'Professor' sounds so formal, and I should like to think we can become friends."

"Behave yourself!" Maggie said to him sternly. "Don't fall for his charm, dear. You call him: Professor Trant."

"You used to be fun, Maggie. You know, Becky, this beauty here would never take 'no' for an answer. There was I, studying for university, and she would be at my door, enticing me out with all types of suggestive things."

"Don't you believe a word of it, my dear! Look, you old charmer, are you going to keep us here at the door - making us listen to a lot of old blarney, or are you going to move yourself so we can come in?"

David hobbled into the front room.

The sight of a whole wall shelved in books made Becky think of Sean and his collection.

"Becky here has got something to show you that I think you'll find interesting. I told her it's your subject."

Becky took the book from her bag and handed it to him.

"Maggie, my girl, would you pass my glasses?" he said, pointing to the table with his walking stick. "Thanks."

Maggie then went off to put the kettle on, leaving them to discuss the book.

He looked at the front cover, then turned it over to see the back. As he opened it, a rancid earthy, smell filled the room.

"Sorry, I should have warned you; it happens every time you open it," Becky said.

"Does it? That's interesting," he said, burying his nose into the pages to have a good sniff. "Can't quite put my finger on that smell, but it tells me it's been around for many centuries." As he browsed through the pages, he said, "I just don't believe what I'm holding! In all my years of studying books on folklore, I've never seen one like this - especially about Balor. If this is genuine, it would make it like the holy grail of books. It's widely known that Balor was just a scary story told to the children, but having this in my hands . . . I think it proves it's more than a story," he said, as he turned the pages. Peering over the top of his glasses, he said with excitement, "Where did you get this?"

As Maggie came into the room with the drinks, she heard the question.

"She lives in the old castle, up on the hill," she said.

"What – 'Caislen Su'l?' You live there?"

"Is that a bad thing or good thing?" Becky asked.

"No, it's just that there's a lot of history attached to it. Where exactly did you find this book?"

"There's a room at the bottom of the castle, that had been blocked up. When it was uncovered, the book was found down there (and a bit more)," Becky replied.

"So when you say: 'a bit more', what exactly are you referring to? Are there more books?" he asked, with a hopeful look.

"It's a long story."

"Well, I have a lot of time on my hands nowadays and, if it's to do with this book, I would like to hear it."

Becky told him about the deaths in the room and her concern that it had something to do with her husband's disappearance.

"Well, that's some story. So, if you say the room was bricked up before your husband's disappearance, and you feel sure that your husband might be in there, that would tell me that there must be another way in."

"I suppose there might be," Becky replied.

"But the question is: where? Look, let me do some research on the place and the surrounding area. May I keep the book meanwhile?"

"Yes, of course; do you want my number?"

"Please."

"Well, David, we'd better get going, in case Tommy Deneen calls back with some news."

"How's the lad doing in the job?" he asked.

"He's still wet behind the ears, and has a long way to go before he's anything like his daddy," Maggie answered.

"Well, we all have to start somewhere."

"Maybe. Anyway, we'll say goodbye. You look after yourself, you old charmer. We'll see ourselves out," Maggie said to him.

"Bye, Professor Trant, and thank you."

"Please, call me David."

"My dear, we are leaving now!" Maggie said, guiding Becky and Finbar out of the room.

As they pulled up at the front door of the castle, they could see Tommy Deneen standing there.

"Have you been here long?" Becky asked, as she got out of the car.

"No. I've only just turned up."

"You go on in, dear, with Tommy. I'll bring the young master in," Maggie said to her.

Becky went on into the kitchen with Tommy.

"So, have you heard anything?" Becky asked, sitting down.

"No, not yet; but I need to ask you a question. Did you know that your husband's father walked out on his family, without any explanation?"

"Yes, I've always known that. You're not going to suggest that, just because his father walked out, he's done the same? He wouldn't do that. He loves me - and Finbar. He wouldn't do that!" she said, starting to cry.

As she came in with Finbar, Maggie noticed her tears; putting him down and walking over to comfort Becky, she said to Tommy, "What do you think you're doing, upsetting her again, you insensitive specimen of a man? Why don't you go back out there and do your job of finding him?"

"Maggie, it's a question that had to be asked; we need to rule out all avenues.

"And how did you find out about that?" Maggie asked him.

"Duffy. He said that Mr Finnegan had told him all about his father leaving him when he was a lad."

"How can you believe a word that comes out of his mouth, when he's always drunk?" Maggie demanded.

"So you saw him?" Becky asked, pulling herself together.

"Yes, I questioned him. He admitted leaving your husband up at the view, but I have a feeling he's holding something back. Rest assured, I haven't finished with him. By the way, I told him that you were waiting to see him and that his friend Maggie was here too. You should have seen his face!" he chuckled.

"I should think so too! That's because he knows what's waiting for him - not coming back last night, keeping us from knowing if Mr Finnegan was there, drinking. Have you still got my old rolling pin in the drawer?" Maggie asked.

"I think I'd better wait here till he gets back; we wouldn't want a murder on our hands, would we, Maggie?"

"I wouldn't waste my time killing him! I'd just try and knock some sense into that empty head of his," she answered.

"Stop it, Maggie; I don't feel like laughing," Becky said, miserably.

"Well, I'll keep you updated if anything turns up. I'll see myself out."

Maggie looked at the wall clock. It had been several hours since Tommy Deneen had left.

"Well, it doesn't look like that gutless waste-of-space is coming back tonight, if at all."

"To be honest, Maggie, I wouldn't mind if Duffy never came back. I didn't relish being here on my own with him. I often said to Sean he gave me the creeps, but he wouldn't have it; he would say he's all right."

"My dear, you're not going to be on your own. I'm here now."

"Maggie, I can't expect you to stay here; you have your own little place to see to."

"Doreen lives next door. I know she'll be keeping an eye on it for me; she's ever so good like that. No, don't you go worrying yourself about that. Now, why don't I make us something to eat, then we can settle down for the night?"

As they ate their meal, Becky asked, "Tell me Maggie was there a Mr . . . I'm sorry, you know - I don't know your surname."

"O'Brien. Yes, I was married. He was a lovely man, Patrick. He treated me like his princess. He passed away eight years and four months ago. (God bless his soul.)"

"So how long were you married?"

"Fifty-three years. It only seems like yesterday! I often think about all the memories of our life together."

"Did you have any children?"

"No. Somehow it just didn't happen. In a way, Master Calon was my child; when I came to live and work at the castle, I took over the role of mothering him. Then when I got married I had a place of my own and, of course, Patrick to look after, so Calon was sent away to boarding school and I made the journey to the castle twice a day. Thankfully, Mr

Finnegan was understanding and let me carry on - he must have liked my cooking," Maggie chuckled. "Well, my dear, I don't know about you, but if you don't mind, I think I'll make my way up to my room."

Becky looked at the clock. "Sorry, Maggie, I didn't realise it was so late, or I wouldn't have asked you all those questions."

"Not at all, my dear. I've enjoyed our little chat. It's not often I get the chance, living on my own."

"Well, I think I'll try to get some rest too."

Maggie looked at Finbar, fast asleep in his cot, and said, "It looks like the young master beat us to it."


Maggie was abruptly woken from her sleep by a scream coming from Becky's room, above her. As fast as her legs would allow, Maggie struggled up the stairs to Becky's bedroom door, but before she had a chance to knock, Becky came rushing out with Finbar in her arms.

"Maggie, Maggie, he was here again!"

"Who, my dear, who?"

"That vile figure! He was standing over Finbar, grinning!"

Not being completely awake, Maggie couldn't make sense of what Becky was saying, but it was clear by the state she was in that something had happened to frighten her.

Becky took Finbar downstairs, with Maggie following.

"Maggie, can we sleep in your room tonight? I'm not sleeping up there again!"

"Of course, my dear; it's a big old bed."

When Becky opened her eyes, the morning sun was shining through the gap in the curtains. Realising it wasn't her room, she remembered what had happened, and turned to see that Maggie and Finbar weren't there. She went down to the kitchen in her nightclothes, to find Finbar being fed by Maggie.

"Morning, my dear; did you sleep well, after last night? You gave me a scare, that you did. I couldn't get up those stairs fast enough!"

"Sorry, Maggie; I didn't mean to scare you, but it was the same as before. I suddenly woke up, knowing that someone was in the room, and when I saw him standing over Finbar, I just screamed."

"Right, sit down. I've just made the tea. Now, tell me word-for-word what you saw."

Becky told her about the night before, and the previous experience.

"You believe me, Maggie, don't you?"

"Of course, my dear. I've never experienced *seeing* anything here, but there have been times when I've been cleaning that room and I thought someone was watching me from by the bookcase. But I just dismissed it as my imagination - being in an old castle. But that's not saying that what *you* saw wasn't real. We need to mention it to David when he contacts us."

"I'm sorry to ask you, Maggie, and make you climb all those stairs, but would you come back with me to get my clothes from that room?"

"Of course, dear; let's just put Finbar in the cot. I'm sure he'll be alright for a few minutes while we get your things."

Having dressed, Becky said, "Maggie, as it's Sunday, do you know if there's a church in the town that I could go to this morning?"

"Well, there's Father Dorian's," she answered.

"No, Maggie, it's Catholic isn't it? I'm a Christian."

"We're all Christians, my dear."

"Well, a Protestant church then."

"There's 'Grace Christian Fellowship' in the square. I hear it's a bit lively."

"Well, I'll give it a try."

"Do you attend church then?" Maggie asked.

"I used to as a child, and I still believe. I just feel that I need to be prayed for."

"Yes, my dear. It's times like this you need the church to comfort you. I always find time to go to mass every Saturday and Sunday."

"Maggie, you should have said yesterday! I'm so sorry to have made you miss it. What time is it today?"

"12 o'clock and 9 o'clock this evening, but I can give it a miss. I'm sure Father Dorian will understand when I tell him."

"No, Maggie. It's important that you go; you've missed yesterday and that's bad enough. No, you've got to go today," Becky insisted.

"I'll tell you what, my dear: you go this morning and I'll stay here and look after the young master, and I'll go to tonight. That way we both get to go to church. Look, you'd better get a move on if you're going to make it to the service. It's not good to walk in late and have everyone look at you, especially being a newcomer."

"Well, if you're sure Maggie."

Becky kissed Finbar good-bye, put on her coat and drove off.

She was greeted by two friendly stewards at the entrance and the service hadn't started, which gave her a chance to look for a seat. People in nearby seats reached over and shook her hand, making her feel welcome and helping her to relax a bit more.

The service started with some worship songs, led by a group of singers and musicians at the front. She'd never heard such modern-sounding songs in a church before, and she found herself listening attentively. Some of the words and music were so beautiful that she felt tears running down her face and she felt as though her heart would break.

A man of about her age then got up to speak and his preaching seemed to draw rapt attention from all the people, but she couldn't stop thinking about Sean and how lonely and lost she felt without him. If only someone could tell her where he was; not knowing was torture and she longed fervently for the nigtmare to end.

Lost in thought, the words, "Would you like to join us for a coffee?" brought her back. It was the woman next to her. She realised that she hadn't heard a word of the pastor's message and now it was over.

"I'm Carley," she said, smiling.

"Hi. I'm Becky."

"I can tell by your accent that you're American. Are you visiting?"

"No, I live here," Becky replied.

"What, here in Bantry?"

"Yes, well not in the town." Becky felt slightly embarrassed to say, "at the castle."

"You live there?"

"Well yes, with my husband."

"That's wonderful! Shall we go for that coffee, and then you can tell me what it's like to live in a castle."

In the coffee lounge they chatted happily. Carley was so warm and friendly that Becky managed to forget the ache in her heart for a while and, although temporary, it was a welcome relief. After a while Carley asked:

"So what did you think of the service? Was it like those in America?"

"Maybe, but not the church I went to – when I was a child. I haven't been for years. No,
this was so much less formal, and the songs!"

"Too loud and lively for you?"

"No, it was the slow ones – they were more like love songs."

"That's exactly what they are . . . "

At that moment the pastor came into the room. Becky overheard someone refer to him as 'Pastor Sean' and the name immediately brought back her pain.

"I must introduce you to our pastor," Carley said, getting up and going over to him.

Pastor Sean was delighted to meet Becky and very interested to hear that she was living in the castle that her husband had inherited. They chatted for a while, but Becky wanted to get to the point without being rude and she could see there was someone waiting to speak to him.

"Pastor, do you have a few minutes so I could talk to you about a private matter?" Becky plucked up the courage to ask.

"Yes, of course. Let me just speak to this person, and we can go somewhere quiet," he replied.

Becky chatted a bit longer with Carley, and found herself hoping they could become good friends.


"I see you've found a friend," the Pastor said to Becky, as he came to their table. "I'm free now if you still want to chat?"

"Becky, here's my number; if you want to get together, give me a ring," Carley said, as Becky got up to go with Pastor Sean.

Sean closed the door. "Well, Becky, what is it you want to talk about?"

Becky explained that she was afraid and felt she needed prayer. She poured out all that had happened since she had arrived in Ireland.

"Well, that's some story. I must confess that, in all the time I've been a pastor, I've never heard anything like that. Of course I'll pray for you – let's bow our heads. As Pastor Sean prayed, Becky felt peace and comfort settle upon her. He prayed that her husband would be found and that she and her family would be protected from evil. He gave her a lovely bookmark with Psalm 91 on it and recommended her to read it whenever she felt afraid. He also assured her that he would keep praying for her and told her she could call him for help any time.

"How did it go, my dear?  Was the church lively enough for you?" Maggie said.

"Yes; it's a lovely, friendly church and the pastor is nice.  He prayed for me."

"I'm pleased, dear.  I was worried about you after last night; how do you feel now?"

"Much better.  How's Finbar been - no trouble I hope?"

"What that little one, no . . . he hasn't got an ounce of trouble in him," Maggie said, stroking his head. Lunch?"


The doorbell rang at 8 o'clock. "That'll be Doreen to take me to mass.  Now, I should be back about 9.30; I usually have a natter after, but I'll come straight back. Bye, dear."

As Maggie made her way up the stairs, Becky called out, "Maggie can you lock the front door and take the key with you, just in case I fall asleep?"

"Of course, my dear."

Becky didn't feel like watching the television and decided to read, so she took Finbar with her to the library.  In front of the great fireplace was a deep cushioned chair where she sat herself down with a book.  After a while, she could feel her eyes closing, but the sound of the front door opening and closing make her snap out of her tiredness.

"You're back early, Maggie," she said, seeing that it was only 9 o'clock. " I'm in the library!" she called out.

But there was no answer.

"Maggie! Is that you?" she called out again.

Then the lights went out, which made her get up out of the chair and face the door. The only light in the room was the moonlight shining through the window, but it enabled her to see the library door slowly opening. Then, to her horror, standing in the doorway was the grotesque figure of the man that had appeared in her room before.

Becky did no more than grab Finbar from his basket and rush out of the other door and up the stairs. There were many rooms off the dark oak-panelled corridor. She could hear his heavy footsteps causing each step to creak as he followed her up the stairs.

She knew she had to hide. She had run past many of the rooms and was near the end of the corridor, so she went into the next room and hid behind the door. The sound of doors opening told her that he was systematically looking in each room.

Then the noises told her he was outside the room next door. She knew it wouldn't be long before he came into the one where she was hiding. She held her breath, hoping he might give up before that and go on to the higher level where her bedroom was. But her hope was dashed by Finbar, who started to cry.

"Shush!" she whispered, stroking his face and desperately trying to quieten him.

She heard the footsteps coming towards her room. The handle started to turn and the door slowly began to open.

Becky's heart was pounding with fear, so much that it was hurting her to breathe. Just as she thought she'd pass out, she heard:

"I'm back, my dear!"

The door stopped opening. She heard the footsteps carry on towards the end of the corridor.

Becky ran out of the room with Finbar and down the stairs.

"Maggie! Maggie! I'm so glad you're home!" she said rushing up to her.

Thinking it was the darkness that had scared her, Maggie said, "What's up with these lights?"

"They went out - just before that man appeared. He was after us, Maggie! If you hadn't come back he would have found us."

"Slow down, dear. What man?"

"The one that was in my room last night," she said, trying to get her breath back.

"Oh my dear - you poor thing! I shouldn't have left you on your own. Where is he now?"

"Upstairs on the first level somewhere. I was hiding in one of the rooms."

"Let's do something about these lights, then I'll go and check up there."

"Do you know where the electrical cupboard is?" Becky asked.

"Oh yes, my dear. There's been many a time when I've had to reset the fuses after a storm. They're in that cupboard there. That's strange - there's nothing wrong with the fuse; the main switch has been turned off. There, now we have light," she said, throwing the main switch.

"I thought you had Duffy to do that kind of thing?" Becky said.

"What him? He wouldn't know where to start! He doesn't know how to light a candle without setting the place on fire; he's useless. I dread to think how poor Mr Finnegan got on when the lights went out after I

left," Maggie said, closing the cupboard door. "But I'll tell you what, my dear, I'm pretty sure that, whoever the man is, he's not a ghost."

"What makes you say that, Maggie?"

"I've never heard of a ghost turning a switch off. I would have thought they could just make the lights go off, without doing that."

"I'm not so sure, Maggie - twice I've seen him disappear."

"Did you actually *see* him do that?" Maggie asked.

"Well, not really - but by the time I turned on the light he had gone. I mean, with the door locked in my room, there was nowhere for him to go. He's got to be a ghost or something supernatural," Becky replied.

"Well, let's see if he's still up there," Maggie said, making her way to the stairs.

"Maggie, please don't wear yourself out tackling those stairs."

"I'm fine. If I take my time I'll be alright."

Becky followed behind. Having reached the landing, Maggie called out, "Right then, whoever you are! If you're up here, I'll find you. If you're not dead, you'll wish you were when I've finished with you!"

Maggie worked her way along, looking in every room until they came to the last one. The pair of them stood poised outside the door.

Becky whispered, "Maggie, do you think he could be in there?"

"We're about to find out. I'll let no man scare me, even if he is a ghost," she said, opening the door quickly.

The room was empty.

"Well, he's not up here; that's for sure, my dear."

"Maybe he's gone up to my room. There's no other place he can be hiding. If he had come back down the stairs he would have had to come past us," Becky said.

Maggie looked at the stairs that led to the upper room; she didn't relish going up them. It must have been obvious, as Becky said:

"Leave it, Maggie – please! They're too much for you."

"If I don't, it won't be only you not sleeping tonight."

"I'm not sleeping in this place tonight! Not now, with that *thing* wandering around. I'd rather sleep in the car!" Becky announced.

"Car! No, my dear, we're going back to my place. It might not be much, compared with this place, but it's safe - that's for sure, and you will have a night's sleep."

"Are you sure, Maggie?"

"I won't hear another word on it," Maggie said.

Becky gathered up Finbar's things and some for herself then they left the place, locking the door behind them.


"Did you sleep well, my dear?

"Yes, thank you; even Finbar didn't wake up in the night."

"Well, there's breakfast on the table when you're ready and then I think it's time we rang David to see if there are any answers about the castle."

"That would be great, Maggie."

# Chapter 13

"David, it's me - Maggie. Becky and I wondered if you've found anything about the castle?"

"Yes, I was going to ring you today to ask if I could visit the place. There's stuff I'd like to check out."

"I'm sure you can," Maggie turned to Becky and relayed his request. They arranged to pick him up in half an hour.


"So this is 'Caislen Su'l?' I've seen it in books but never had the time or the opportunity to visit."

"Will you be alright getting down these stairs, Professor Trant?" Becky asked.

"I'll be fine; I'll take my time," David replied.

"Please take a seat and you can tell me what you've found out."

Maggie busied herself making some drinks, but listened to what he had to say.

Professor Trant took the book from his shoulder bag and put it on the table.

"Well, firstly: the book is genuinely old. A young friend of mine, who works at the university, came over and took it away for testing. He reckons it to be over 3,000 years old."

"What that book? It can't be. How come it's so well preserved?" Becky asked, amazed.

"A very good question! We couldn't at first make out what the cover and pages were made of. We know that early writings were done on papyrus, wood or slate, and later parchment (that's prepared animal skins). We could see it wasn't any of the first three, so we thought it had to be some sort of parchment. But then we dismissed that as well, because of its age. Then, after doing some further tests, we had a bit of a shock. This book *is* made from skin, but not from an animal. It is mummified human skin. Now, don't freak out, but the ink is blood.

"Ugh . . . That's *horrible* - and to think I've handled it! Is that why it has an awful smell?"

"That's a mystery. I would have thought, after all these years, the smell of decomposing flesh would have gone, but somehow it's lingered."

"How would they have got all that skin?" Becky asked.

"Not from volunteers, that's for sure," he answered. "Whoever made it must have stuck layers and layers of skin together, to get the thickness of the cover and pages."

"So, do you think it's one of the oldest books ever to be found?" Becky asked.

"Well, up to now, the oldest one was thought to be: the Etruscan Gold Book, which was discovered seventy years ago, whilst digging a canal off the Strouma River in Bulgaria. It's made from six sheets

of 24-carat gold, bound together with rings. The plates are written in Etruscan characters, with depictions of a horse and horseman, plus a siren, lyre, and soldiers."

"I've never heard of the Etruscans," Becky said.

"Etruscans were an ancient race of people that migrated from Lydia – now modern Turkey – settling in central Italy nearly three thousand years ago. I guess this book tops that," he said excitedly.

"I thought the Bible was the oldest?" Becky replied.

"You mean the Dead Sea Scrolls? No, they're just over two thousand."

"So did you and your friend know what language this book is and what those weird symbols throughout mean?"

"We think it is an ancient form of Gaelic. We could work out some of the words. It tells of a race of people called the 'Fomorians', who invaded the land. I'm toying with the idea that, because of the symbols, it might be the book of a Druid high priest."

"I've lived here all my life and I've never heard of the Fomorians," said Maggie, interested in what David was saying.

"This was long before your time, Maggie! In Irish-Celtic mythology, the Fomorians were a race of demonic giants, ancient occupants of Ireland (or sometimes mentioned as a mythical, prehistoric people who raided and pillaged Ireland from the sea). They were a fearsome race, as many invaders found out. So you can see why I'm excited about this book. Up to now, Balor has been just a myth."

"So, Professor Trant, who (or what) is 'Balor'?" Becky asked.

"Well, according to forklore, Balor was the Fomorian's greatest champion, and their leader. He was also known as 'the god of death'. He only had one eye, which was usually closed. It's said that its gaze killed anyone that saw it, thus he became known as 'Balor of the Evil Eye'. The story goes that, as a youngster, after spying on druids preparing a draught of wisdom, some of the potion splashed into to his eye, which made his stare baleful to all those he looked upon. He kept his evil eye closed when not in battle, and his lid was so heavy that he needed four attendants to lift it."

"I can see why it's just a story told to the children," Becky said.

"Yes, that's folklore for you. Anyway, Balor apparently hears a prophecy that he will be killed by his grandson. To avoid this fate, he locks his only daughter, Ethniu, in a tower on Tory Island to keep her from becoming pregnant. However, Cian, with the help of the druidess, Birog, manages to enter the tower. He seduces her and she gives birth to a son (Lugh), but Balor throws him into the ocean. Birog saves Lugh and gives him to Manannan mac Lir, who becomes his foster father.

As time goes on, Lugh grows to be a mighty warrior and confronts Balor on the battlefield and, with a stone flung from his sling, kills him."

"That's like the story of the young Israelite, David, killing Goliath."

"That's right, my young lovely," he said. Apparently Lugh takes out Balor's eye and buries it under a huge stone, so nobody could ever dig it up and use the magic. For it was believed that whoever had the eye would have the evil power of the Druids."

"We have a big stone here in the grounds," Becky announced.

"There are lots of them throughout Ireland and, remember, this is only a story passed down," he replied to her.

"Yes, but funnily enough, I noticed this one because it has an eye carved on it."

"Are you sure it's an eye?" he asked.

"Yes, I'm sure. It looks very much like the eye on the book cover."

"I would like to see it, if that's okay?"

"Of course you can, Professor Trant, that's why you're here. So were you able to decipher any more of the book?"

"Yes, it tells of a place called the 'Cave of Balor', and in there at the Summer Solstice and Winter Equinox they would take chosen people from the village to be sacrificed and have their eyes removed and offered to Balor. If the eyes were accepted by him, they believed that they would share his magical powers in the afterlife. The Druids would record every eye removed by carving an eye shape into the rock wall. So, tell me, where's the room the book was found in?" he asked.

"Behind that dresser," Becky said pointing. "If it's of any interest, I found in the library here an old book on the castle."

"Yes. It might give us a bit more information."

"Maggie, would you mind looking after Finbar while I show Professor Trant the library?"

"Not at all my dear, you go on."

As Becky opened the library door, she was confronted by an unexpected sight. Every book had been thrown to the floor.

"What happened here?" the professor asked. "It looks as if someone was searching for something."

"I think he was looking for the book we have," Becky said.

"Who's 'he'?"

"He is the reason we didn't stay here last night. Three times since living here I've seen a hideous figure, twice in my bedroom and once here in the library. Both times in the bedroom he disappeared before I could get the light on, and when I was in here he followed me upstairs, then disappeared when Maggie came through the front door."

"What did he look like?" he asked.

"Fat and stocky with a horrible face and he only had one eye."

The professor reached into his bag and took out a book. "Something like this?" he said, showing her a picture.

"That's him! Even the clothes! Who is it?" Becky asked, not taking her eyes from the picture.

"Balor," he replied.

"How can that be?" gasped Becky.

"All I know is, there have been a lot of unexplained, weird things that have been seen, and anything to do with Druids and their ancient magic, well . . ."

"Are you saying that Balor's ghost roams this castle?"

"I don't know about 'ghost', but the question is: what is the connection between the castle and Balor?

You said you had an old book about the castle in here?"

"Yes, it was up there on the top shelf with the book of the Finnegans, but now it could be anywhere amongst this lot," she said looking at the floor.

"Well, there's only one way to find out. If you pick them up, I'll re- stack them. It's a wicked thing to treat old books like this."

"I didn't realise there were so many subjects," Becky said.

"Yes, there is quite a variety; they say that you can tell a lot about a person by what they read," he replied.

"I've found it! Oh look, and the other one about the Finnegans," Becky said excitedly. "Shall I put them on this table or would you like to take them back to the kitchen?"

"No, on the table here will be fine."

The professor put on his glasses and opened the book about the castle.

"So much more information – now we know when it was first built," he said, thumbing through it eagerly.

"So how old is it, Professor?"

"It says it was built by the Normans in 1175, which is a hundred years older than previously thought."

"Is there any reference to what was here before that?"

"Why do you say that?"

"Well, for a start, the big stone. I know it's a lot older than the castle and for the stone to have been put there, the place must have had some importance."

"Oh yes? So how do you know this?"

"Duffy told me. (We kind of inherited him with the castle.) And then I was reading that

maybe there was a fortified structure here."

"You've certainly done your research! You're probably right: the position - being high up, looking out to sea and the surrounding land, is ideal. They would have seen any invader for miles."

"So, there's no actual reference to what was here before?" she asked.

"No, but there are drawings of the castle's structure which show the lower west wall was built into solid rock. (I think that's where the kitchen is.) It was probably a dungeon or the castle vaults originally, but more importantly, the lower room that you bricked up must have been some sort of cave."

"Wow!"

"We won't know for sure until we find the other entrance, if there is one. Can I have a look at the Finnegan book? It might give us a little more information."

"Yes, of course."

The professor opened the book and started to read. "Have you read this?"

"No, why?"

"It's a daily diary of the Finnegans that have lived here, starting with Finbar Finnegan. He apparently bought it in ruins in 1860. He employed a lot of local men to help restore it. When it was finished, he called it: 'Finnegan Castle'! He can't do that!" he said, alarmed.

"Well, he did. What's wrong with that?" Becky asked, surprised.

"It's meddling with history! These people think, just because they have money, they can do what they like," he said crossly.

"Professor Trant, these so called 'people' are my husband's relatives," she said, quietly.

"Of course. Sorry, it's just that I get so irritated when I come across things like this."

He carried on reading. "Ah! See, it says that Duffy, his servant, told him that by changing the name he would evoke a curse on his family name and every firstborn son would die."

"That must be *our* Duffy's ancestor; he told us that his family served the Finnegans. Where would he have got that information about a curse from?" Becky asked.

"I should imagine, being a local, he might have said it because he didn't like the idea of the castle's name being changed. Maybe *he* invoked the curse."

"It makes you wonder if curses are real and not just mumbo jumbo."

"It's a fascinating subject," he replied.

"Professor Trant, come over here and look at this - it's a family tree of the Finnegans. I was studying it the other day and I worked out that the firstborn sons *did* die, and Sean, my husband, is the first born of Calon, in fact his only son. If he is dead, that tells me the curse is still alive," she said, holding back tears.

Seeing that she was upset, Professor Trant held her hand and said, "We don't know for sure that he's dead, now do we?"

"I suppose not," she replied.

He carried on studying the family tree. "Mmm . . . very interesting. Someone's written here that a curse can only be effective if you believe in it," he said.

"Well, Finbar Finnegan must have. But I know for sure Sean doesn't so that reassures me that, wherever he is, he's okay."

215

"Let's hope so," he replied, sounding more confident than he felt. He went back to reading the book.

"It's a shame some of the pages have been removed."

"Why would someone want to do that?" Becky asked.

"Who knows, maybe someone didn't want the contents to be seen."

"I think I remember Duffy telling us something about that. Now, who was it he was talking about? Yes - Sean's grandfather! He said that he noticed that the pages had been torn out. And there was reference to the room in the book. Have you come across that yet?"

"No . . . Ah, here it is," he said, going back a few pages. "I don't know how I missed that. Yes, it says, '*After the death of Daniel, I had the room walled up so nothing evil like that could happen again.*' It doesn't say who made the entry, but it's in a different handwriting. I suspect it was his wife."

"Does it say anything else?"

"No, that's the last entry and, as far as I can see, that's the only reference in it to the room. It does sound like something's been going on down there. I need to explore outside to see if there is another way into it, starting with that big stone."

"As it's a bit of an up-hill walk, why don't I drive you up there? I'll just go and tell Maggie where we're going."

"Yes, that's fine; I'll stay here."

While she was gone, he studied the paintings of the Finnegans, especially the one of Finbar, above the great fireplace. He noticed that it was slightly

crooked and couldn't resist reaching up to straighten it. He managed to push one end up, and as he did so, something fell to the ground. It appeared to be some folded pieces of paper, which had obviously been hidden there. Struggling, he reached down to pick them up and sat down at the table to examine them. As he unfolded them, he realised they were the missing pages of the Finnegan Diary.

"I'm ready," Becky said, coming in with the car keys in her hand.

"Come and see what I found behind one of the paintings," he said, beckoning her over.

"What is it?" she said eagerly.

"The missing pages!" he said, replacing them in the book. "We were right; there is another entrance to the room. Apparently, it's behind the big stone; and there's a sketch showing that, during the Summer Solstice and Winter Equinox, you can see the sun striking the stone - from the castle tower. It says that a shadow shows the alignment to the castle."

"Let's go and find it!" she said, rushing off to the car and forgetting he wasn't able to walk as fast as her.

The professor eventually caught up, and Becky's car spun the gravel on the drive as she drove off to the stone.

The professor stood in front of the stone and turned, in an effort to see the alignment. He noticed that, even though there was a downhill gradient, there was a clear straight line to the lefthand side of the castle, where the kitchen was.

"Have a look at the eye on the stone, Professor," Becky said.

"I see what you mean. Even though it's very worn and weathered, it looks just like the one on the book cover."

In the typical manner of a professional, he took his time taking in every detail, while Becky was impatiently looking amongst the bushes and rocks for the entrance.

She went back to the professor, who was now writing and sketching in his book.

"I can't see anything that resembles an entrance."

"Well, I shouldn't think it'll be staring us in the face. These sorts of things were designed to be hidden. Let me have a look."

He stood behind the stone and faced the castle. "Now if we line this position up with the castle and look directly behind us . . . we should be looking . . . here!" he exclaimed.

With his walking stick he pushed back the branches of a bush.

"See, Becky - that pile of stones, it's not natural."

"How do you know that? It looks like a normal pile of stones to me."

"That's what it's supposed to do. No, if it was, you would see moss or grass growing in between the stones."

"I see," she said having a closer look. "So let's dismantle them," she said, trying to lift the top stone.

"Becky, they're too heavy for you and I can't do it, with this hip. I'm afraid we'll have to leave it until you find someone who can."

"That's so disappointing - we're so close," she said, trying once more.

"Well, at least we've found it. We can come back another day. I'm sorry - I have to get back. I'm expecting a phone call around tea time."

"Yes, I don't want to be anywhere near this place when it's dark."


"How did you get on? Did you find what you were looking for?" Maggie asked, as they came into the kitchen.

"Yes, Maggie, we did. We found the entrance to the room!" Becky announced with enthusiasm. "But we had to leave it as we couldn't move the pile of stones at the entrance. If that Duffy was here he could have done it. He's never around when you want him. Where is he anyway?" Becky said in exasperation.

"That's him for you, my dear! As I said, a useless specimen. I tell you, now he knows I'm here, we won't be seeing his face," Maggie replied.

"I'm sorry to rush you two, but I have to leave now if I'm to be on time for that call."

"Yes, Maggie, he's got to get back and we have to get out of here before it's dark. I'm not staying here. Sorry - I'm taking it for granted that it's all right to stay at your place again. Is it okay?"

"Of course, my dear. I told you - you can stay as long as you like. Look, you help him up the stairs and I'll bring the young master up."


"Thank you, Professor Trant, for today," Becky said, pulling up outside his house.

"No - thank *you*. I've had a rewarding day. If I find anything more about the place, I'll let you know. Is it alright if I hang on to the book for a bit longer?"

"Of course. I don't want anything to do with it (now I know what it's made of), or the castle. You go and take your call. Bye for now."

On the way back to Maggie's, Becky said to her, "Your friend, the policeman's wife, do you think you could ring her and ask if he could come and see me?"

"There's no need, she lives next door."

"Of course - you said that."

"Is it about what you found out today?"

"Yes, it might help with finding Sean. I've got to try anything, even if it all leads nowhere."

"Of course you have, my dear."


"Maggie! It's only me!" a voice called from the back door.

"In here, Tommy!" Maggie called back.

"Evening to you both. Doreen said that you wanted to speak to me, Mrs Finnegan. I take it it's about your missing husband? I'm sorry, we still haven't had any clues on his whereabouts."

"Well, that's what I want to talk about. I was up at the castle today with Professor Trant; it's about something we found," Becky said.

"Professor Trant?" he replied, never having heard of him.

"Your daddy knew him, Tommy; he's a professor, or was, at the university," Maggie told him.

"No, can't say that I know him."

"Well anyway, we went to see him the other day about an old book that was found at the castle.

220

Apparently, it revealed that the room downstairs (where my husband's father and grandfather died) was an old Druid cave - where they sacrificed people."

"Mrs Finnegan, are you saying that's got something to do with their deaths?"

"They weren't the only two. Professor Trant found an entry in the family diary saying that a 'Daniel Finnegan' died in there as well."

"I didn't hear about that. When was it?"

"You wouldn't have - it was 1937," she replied.

"1937! I was going to say, a death here that I didn't know anything about."

"And there were three other Finnegans that died suddenly at the castle."

"What in that room?" he asked, surprised.

"Well, I don't know for sure, but I have a strong feeling they did. All I do know is that they were all first-born sons."

"What's that got to do with them dying? I'm sorry, Mrs Finnegan, but you must understand my job is to deal with hard facts and proof, not old stories from Druid days. Is this what you wanted to talk to me about?

"No! No, I know all this sounds silly and far-fetched, but I have a feeling that my husband may have died in there too."

"Mrs Finnegan, didn't you say that you had the room bricked up before he went missing?"

"I know I did, but I just know somehow he's in there."

"Well, I just have to ask: how do you think he got in there then?"

221

"That's what I want to talk to you about. The professor has found another entrance to the room - up by the big stone in the grounds."

"Another entrance you say? What makes you sure it's the entrance to the room?"

"It was in the missing pages of the book," she said, getting flustered.

"I'm sorry, Mrs Finnegan. I've had a long shift today, but I'm missing something here. What missing pages? What book?"

Maggie could see that Becky wasn't explaining herself very well, and everyone was getting tired, so she said, "Look, Tommy, why don't you call in tomorrow morning and you two can go up to the castle, then she can show you what she has been trying to tell you. I think that would be better."

With a sigh of relief, he replied, "Yes, okay. I'm not on till the evening shift, so I'll be able to do that. I'll say goodnight to you all."

"Oh, Maggie, he must have thought I was some crazy woman!"

"No, my dear; they're used to all sorts of strange stories. It will all become clear to him tomorrow - you wait and see. Now let's turn in."


On the way, Tommy asked, "Tell me, Mrs Finnegan, why are you staying with Maggie when you've got that big place?"

Scared that, if she told him the truth, he would think she was a crackpot, Becky wasn't sure how to answer him, especially after the previous evening. "Maggie has been keeping me company these last few days."

"Makes sense," he replied, realising how devastated she must be over her missing husband.

As they drove down the drive to the castle, Tommy said, "I noticed the big stone over there. Didn't you want to show me the entrance you spoke about?"

"Well . . . yes, but can I show you the diary and torn out pages first? It will explain what I've been trying to tell you," Becky replied.

"Sure . . ."

Becky unlocked the big doors and took him into the library.

"Have you had an intruder?" he said, seeing the books all over the floor.

"It's all to do with *him* looking for the book that was found in the downstairs room. It's over here on the table - I want to show you," she said.

"Who are you referring to when you say '*him*'?

"Well it will be easier to show you than try to tell you," she replied, walking over to the table, only to find that the book wasn't there.

"Oh no! Of course, Professor Trant still has the book about Balor! It would have explained all about the cellar room," she said, disappointed that she couldn't show him.

"Did you say: 'Balor'? Please don't tell me that you think he has something to do with all this? With all due respect, Mrs Finnegan, Balor is just an old Irish story."

"I know he is, or was, but the book Professor Trant has proves otherwise. You have to believe me - I've seen him three times here in the castle," she said desperately, trying to make him believe her.

"Mrs Finnegan, the worry of not knowing where your husband is, along with no sleep, can do all sorts of things to a person's mind."

Becky knew that it was futile trying to convince him, and was worried that he'd leave, so decided to say no more.

"You're probably right; I haven't been sleeping. But can I show you the pages inside this diary of the Finnegans, that tell about the entrance up at the stone?"

Becky opened the book, expecting to see the loose pages, but they were gone.

"I don't understand, we left them in the book!"

"Maybe your Professor Trant has them?"

"I know he left them there. He put them back in the place where they were torn out. Honestly, I watched him do it."

"Maybe Balor took them, Mrs Finnegan," he chuckled. "So what is this book?" he said, opening it and browsing through it.

Becky now knew there was no chance of him believing her. "It's a diary of the Finnegans that lived here, and those missing pages show the whereabouts of the entrance to the room. Well, we don't need them, if you let me show you. I can prove that the entrance exists, in case you don't believe me about that either."


"Okay, Mrs Finnegan, let's have a look," he said, glancing at his watch.

"It's just through these bushes," she said, leading the way. "There - see, it's behind that pile of stones."

"They're just rocks, Mrs Finnegan; been there for ever, I should imagine."

"No, the professor pointed out that because there's no moss or grass between the stones, the pile hasn't been there that long. I tried to lift them but they're too heavy for me, but you could, couldn't you?" she asked.

"Can't you get that Duffy to do it?" Tommy replied, not wanting to get his hands dirty.

"I haven't seen him since you told him that Maggie and I were waiting for him."

"But that was last week! Is that normal?" he asked.

"I've known him to be gone a day, but not this long. He can't be *that* scared of Maggie, surely?"

"Wouldn't think so. I'll ask Danny if he's seen him. I can't see him going longer than a day without a drink."

"He told me he sometimes stays with his friend, Angus, but I don't know where that is," Becky replied.

"I know Angus; I'll see if he's there."

"Please, do you think you might be able to move just one of the stones, to see what's behind it?"

Tommy knew he wasn't going to get any peace so, even if it was just to prove there was nothing behind them, it would be worth getting his hands dirty. He lifted one end of the top stone and eased it forward until it toppled off the stone below. He could see already that it revealed an opening.

"It appears you were right, Mrs Finnegan. There is something here."

"Can you see in there?" Becky said hopefully.

"No," he said, trying to peer into the dark void. "But whatever's in there, there's a rank smell of flesh

decomposing - I've smelt it before. I'll have to get the right people here to investigate."

Becky caught a whiff of the odour. That's the same smell as the book gives off. It's horrible! Professor Trant says he thinks the pages are made from mummified skin."

Tommy couldn't believe what he was hearing.

"Okay, Mrs Finnegan, we'll look into it. I'll get back to the station and see if they can get a team up here tomorrow."


"Evening, Tommy. As you're in uniform, I won't ask if you want one. Business is it then?"

"No not really, Danny. Has Duffy been in lately?" Tommy asked.

"You know what, no - he hasn't and that's not like him. Let me see, when did I last see him . . .? Saturday! That was it. You were here asking him questions about that young Finnegan. I knew something was wrong with him because he started on the old poteen and for sure it wasn't because of Maggie O'Brien, I can tell you. No, that was the last time I saw him. Do you think he's ended up in the same ditch as Mrs Malone's old cow? To be sure, it's a deep ditch; to think of poor old Duffy in that ditch and being desperate for a drink," Danny chuckled.

Tommy chuckled too at the thought of it. "Well if you do see him, tell him he had better get his backside up to the castle, if he still wants his job."

"Have you been to Angus's?" Danny asked.

"I thought I'd look in on my way to the castle."

"I hope you find him - the place isn't the same without him!" Danny called as Tommy left.

"Angus, it's me - Tommy Deneen!  You in there?" he called, knocking on the door.

"I has nothing to do with that crate of beer from Raffety's bar," he called back.

"I know nothing about that; all I want to know is: have you seen Duffy lately?"

"No; I was wondering what happened to my old drinking pal.  Can't help you," he called back through the door.

"Okay, Angus.  That's all I wanted to know, and thanks for the information on the crate of beer.  Don't drink it all at once!"

# Chapter 14

Tommy looked at his watch. The team would be waiting for him outside the castle gates.

"Morning, Aaron. Who's the lad then?"

"Morning, Tommy. This here's Brodie, our newest member of the team - just started this morning. The Sarge said that you think there's a decomposing body here in a tunnel, or something?" Aaron replied.

"It might be. I'm not usually wrong; it's a very distinctive smell. I think you'll agree when you smell it. Follow me - it's up by that big stone over there," Tommy said.

Tommy led them through the bushes. "That's strange! That top stone has been put back. Someone has been here, that's for sure."

Brodie went to work, taking photographs of the stones.

"If you take one end, it will be easier," Tommy said to Aaron.

As each stone was removed, the entrance became clearer.

"I see what you mean, Tommy, about the smell! There's definitely a body somewhere in there," Aaron said.

"Judging by the size of that opening, it looks like one-at-a-time going in there then. Good job the Sarge is not with us - he'd never have got in there," Brodie said, with a grin.

"I take it you don't want a career in the Force, then Brodie?" said Tommy.

"I was only making a joke!" Brodie protested.

"You know, we will have to report back to him what you said," Aaron warned.

"No . . . I need this job! My Ma will give me hell if I go back and tell her I've lost my job."

Tommy and Aaron burst into laughter.

"So which of you is going in first?" Tommy said.

"Looks dark in there! I say, as you discovered it, Tommy, it should be you," Aaron said.

Brodie nodded his head, "I agree with that; yep, it should be you, Tommy."

As much as he didn't relish the thought of what might be lurking in there, Tommy knew he didn't have a choice. He crawled through the opening, shining his torch ahead.

"Anything in there, Tommy?" Aaron called after him.

There was no reply.

"Tommy, you all right in there? Speak to me, man!" Aaron shouted, starting to get concerned.

"You'd better go in there after him, Brodie."

"Why me?"

"Well now, Brodie, you see - there's me and there's you. Now, if I went in there, how would you

learn about handling a situation? You wouldn't. So, out of the kindness of my heart, I'm letting *you* go."

"It's just because I'm new that your making me go in there. It's not fair I tell you."

"Stop complaining and get in there! For all we know, whatever's in there has done Tommy in."

"Oh thanks," Brodie said, getting on his hands and knees. "Tommy, you there?" he whispered, as he crawled in. Once through the opening, he found that he was able to stand up, but it was pitch black.

"Did you find him, Brodie?" came Aaron's voice from outside.

"Give me a chance! It's dark in here. Pass me the torch through; I forgot it," Brodie called back.

As Brodie got back on his hands and knees with his head looking out of the opening, he felt a hand on his back.

"Mother of the saints, he's got me!" Brodie screamed, as he scrambled out, banging his head on the rock above. While Aaron helped him to his feet, Tommy emerged.

"It was you! You scared the life out of me, that you did!" Brodie wailed.

"Of course it's me! Who did you think it was, lad?" Tommy chuckled.

"To be sure, it's no laughing matter, Tommy! I thought I was a goner, like you," Brodie complained.

Aaron eventually stopped laughing and said, "So in all seriousness, Tommy, did you see anything in there?"

"The further I got, the stronger the smell was. I went as far as I could go. It ends in front of a big, flat rock with iron rings attached to it. I think the source of the smell is coming from the other side, in which case

I think that big stone is hiding whatever is decomposing. If *you* go in there you might figure out how to move it, Aaron."

"Brodie, go back to the van and get the big floodlight. I need as much light in there as possible," Aaron ordered.

Armed with the floodlight, one by one they all went back into the tunnel.

"This place must be old. I reckon with all these alcoves in here, there's a lot of places to hide. Is it natural or did someone dig it?" Brodie asked.

"Couldn't tell you, lad; all I know is, with the smell of a decomposing body, it looks like a crime scene," Tommy answered. He stopped and bent down to pick up a beer bottle. "It looks like whoever is involved likes their drink."

"You shouldn't have picked it up! Whoever it belongs to would probably have left their prints on it, and you could have smudged them with yours. If you see anything else just tell me," Aaron said.

"Sorry," Tommy said.

"Look there's lots over here!" Brodie said, shining the floodlight on them.

Tommy couldn't help noticing the name on the labels.

"Something of interest?" Aaron asked.

"Maybe. It's something that came up the other day at Murphy's Bar about a certain person drinking nothing but this brew."

"Well don't touch them!" Aaron reminded him.

"I know, prints!" Tommy responded.

"I see what you mean by the stone; what on earth is the purpose of the rings?" Aaron said, studying them and running his hand around the outer edges of

the stone. "As I suspected, somehow this stone moves."

"How do you work that out?" Brodie asked.

Aaron bent down. "Look at the grooves on the floor; you can see that they're caused by this big stone opening towards us; but the question is, lad, how?"

Brodie was close behind Aaron, looking over his shoulder. He took a step backwards quickly as Aaron stood up, but not quickly enough. He lost his balance and reached behind to the wall, trying to steady himself. As he did so, his hand pushed a stone that slid back into the wall. The big stone started to swing open towards them.

"What did you do?"

"I don't know, Aaron, honestly!" Brodie answered, thinking he had done something wrong.

"You're not in trouble, lad. I was just curious. Look, pass the floodlight over, and lets see what's in here."

The beam of the floodlight revealed a vaulted cave.

"Look there's the source of the smell! You were right, Tommy - it's a body," Aaron said.

"Oh, I see," Tommy said, looking around. "I know this place; this is where the last two Finnegans died. It's the cellar room of the castle. I had no idea that this stone moved, but then I had no reason to suspect it did – nor did the forensic team at the time. And this must be Sean Finnegan. Mrs Finnegan was right. I think if you take a closer look, you'll see that his eyes have been removed."

Brodie crouched down to have a closer look. "Yes, how did you know that?"

"Because the other two had theirs' removed."

Brodie began to retch and ran out, back into the tunnel.

"He'll get used to it. Seems like we're dealing with a serial killer who collects eyes," Aaron said.

"Aagh! Aaagh!" came from the tunnel.

The pair of them looked around to see the stone door closing on them. Tommy ran to the door and, with all his might, tried to stop it. Aaron just stood there not fully comprehending what was happening.

"Aaron, I can't hold it! I need help! If this closes on us we'll be trapped in here!"

Aaron raced over to join Tommy. Even with two of them, their strength was inadequate, for whoever was on the other side pushing was stronger than them.

"Aaron, can you reach the floodlight?"

"I think so," he replied.

"See if you can jam it in the opening," Tommy said.

Aaron quickly did so. The steel casing of the light started to crush, shattering the light, but it was enough to stop the stone door from completely closing. The two of them stood with their backs to the door, out of breath, but above the sound of their heavy breathing they could hear the sound of footsteps running along the tunnel.

The two of them pushed the stone open, to see Brodie on the ground, holding his head and moaning.

"I'll see to Brodie, you get after *him,*" Aaron said to Tommy.

Tommy ran along the tunnel with a torch, but was only in time to see a pair of legs scrambling out of the opening.

"So what happened?" Aaron asked Brodie.

"I knew I was going to be sick, so I went over to the alcove here. I was bending over, retching, when I saw a pair of boots in front of me. I looked up and there was this one-eyed, ugly-looking guy grinning at me. Before I knew what was happening, he picked me up and threw me against the wall. The next thing I knew was coming round and seeing you. Where did he come from?"

"He must have been hiding in here somewhere. This alcove goes back some way, he said, shining his torch. "Look, I've got to go and see if Tommy needs help. He's gone after the guy. Are you fit enough to make your way out to the van on your own?"

"I'm not staying here on my own; fit or not, I'm coming with you," Brodie replied.

"I'll have to get going, Maggie, I need to get to the castle and see what's going on. I'll be back as soon as I can."

"Good luck, my dear; let's hope the entrance does lead to that room."

"I hope so, Maggie."

Becky drove through the iron gates and was halfway along the avenue of trees, when a figure suddenly rushed out of the trees onto the drive. There was a screechig of tyres as she slammed on the brakes, but it had all happened too fast for her to stop in time. There was a loud thud and then she saw a body flying through the air towards the windscreen and slide down the bonnet. She rushed out of the car to see the figure lying in a crumbled heap in front of

the vehicle, and Tommy coming out of the trees. The man tried to get up and collapsed.

"Don't try to move," Tommy said. There was no response.

"I didn't have a chance - he came out of nowhere!" Becky said, deeply shocked.

Tommy bent down to check the man, who was laying face down. He gently felt for a pulse.

"Is he dead?" Becky asked.

"No, but I think he won't be running far now."

"Who is he? What was he doing here?" she asked.

"I'll explain in a minute, Mrs Finnegan. I need to phone for an ambulance."

"Shouldn't we cover him? I have a rug in the back of the car."

"It wouldn't hurt," he replied.

"I see he didn't get far!" exclaimed Aaron, making his way towards them.

"How's the lad?" Tommy asked.

"He'll be alright. He's sitting in the van - probably have a sore head for a few days. So, do we know who this fellow is?" Aaron asked.

"We'll get a better look at him when the paramedics arrive and move him. If it hadn't been for Mrs Finnegan here, he'd probably have got away, having the head start that he did. What I don't understand is: why he ran on to the drive towards the castle. It doesn't make sense to run that way - there's no way out."

"Maybe he thought he could hide in the old place. I should think there are plenty of nooks and crannies to hide," Aaron said.

"Are there, Mrs Finnegan?" Tommy asked.

Becky didn't answer. She was staring down at the person lying on the road. Realising that she was in shock, Tommy said, "Mrs Finnegan, you'd be better to go and sit in the car." She didn't move. Tommy placed his hand on her arm.

"Mrs Finnegan! Let's get you in the car."

The ambulance pulled up behind, and the two paramedics walked over to Tommy.

"Do we know who he his?" one of them asked as he knelt down to examine the casualty.

"No not yet," Tommy replied.

"Looks as if nothing's broken - which surprises me, looking at the state of the front of that car. I can't say about his head until we get him back."

I've got a colleague sitting in the van, up by that big stone; he could do with a check over - had a crack on the head," Aaron said to the paramedics.

"Okay; we'll just see to this one. Right, let's see if we can gently turn him over onto the stretcher."

As they turned him over he groaned and opened his eyes.

"Can you tell me your name?" the paramedic asked.

He stared at them without saying anything.

"I'm not a hundred percent sure, but I think that looks something like Duffy," Tommy said, scratching his chin.

Hearing the name 'Duffy', Becky got out of the car.

"Oh no! I've knocked Duffy over - that poor man!"

"So it *is* him?"

Becky stood over him. "I think so.... The hair looks wilder, but the features look like Duffy's."

237

As soon as she said that, one of his eyes started to close and the expression on his face started changing.

"It's the man who was in my room!" Becky gasped, stepping back.

A grin came upon the man's face and with a deep, gutteral voice, he said, "I am Balor, King of the Fomorians! You mere mortals will have no hold on me!" He sat up, ripping away the safety straps that held him there. Jumping from the stretcher, he ran towards the castle.

"What was *that*?" the paramedic exclaimed.

There was silence as they stood there, not believing what had just happened.

"That *was* Duffy wasn't it, Mrs Finnegan?"

"I.... I'm not sure now who, or *what* it was."

"You going after him, Tommy?" Aaron said.

"No, not on my own - with his strength! Did you see how he snapped those straps as if they were made of wool? And look how we struggled, trying to stop him closing that stone on us. He must have the strength of *four* men!"

"Aye, Brodie said he picked him up like a rag doll and threw him from one side to the other. He can't be human, can he?" Aaron said.

Tommy got on his radio, "Sarge, we're going to need back up here - and plenty of it, right away!"

It wasn't long before the sound of sirens came screeching through the iron gates.

"What we got then, Tommy, a cat stuck up a tree?" Brandon said, getting out of the car.

"Very funny, Brandon! The guy's run off and hid in the castle. When you meet him, I'd like to see if you're as funny as you are now."

"What - all these men just for one man?" Brandon replied.

"He might only be one, but I don't know if you could call him a man."

"What do you mean by that, Tommy?"

"You'll see."

"Okay guys, let's go and sort him out."

"You'll let me know when you have him? I need to take Mrs Finnegan home."

"You not coming then, Tommy?"

"What? You need me as well - *just for one man*?" Tommy said with a wry smile. "Don't forget your Tasers. I think you'll need them!" he called out as he went.

Brandon looked back at Tommy. "Pat, go back and get the Taser," he said to his colleague.

"We'll let them find him, Mrs Finnegan, then we can make our way to the castle and maybe make a cup of tea. I need to talk you," Tommy said.

"You know, Officer Deneen, I have a feeling they won't find him in there."

"Why do you say that, Mrs Finnegan?"

"Only that I've seen him appear and disappear in places where it was impossible to hide."

"Mrs Finnegan, I think you'll find that this is not a supernatural being, but Duffy who has had one too many to drink."

"How can you say that, when you witnessed what he did with those straps? And that weird voice that came out of him? It sounds to me as if he is possessed."

239

"Mrs Finnegan, I'm sorry but I just can't believe in stuff like that. I choose to think its just Duffy - a mere drunk."

"Let's hope it is then, Officer Deneen," Becky sighed. "How long do you think they will look for him? I could do with that tea, after a shock like that."

"With all those men, not long. Aaron, when Brandon rings me, can you tidy up here with the paperwork?"

"Yeah, sure. It's best that I wait here anyway - for the forensic guys to come, otherwise they'll never find the body."

"Body? No ... you found him!" Becky gasped, assuming the body was Sean's.

Tommy hadn't wanted her to find out like that. He said, "Look as soon as I get the all-clear we will have that tea."

"It *is* him, isn't it?" she asked, trembling.

"We don't know for sure, Mrs Finnegan; it could be anyone. There's no need to be getting upset until the men get him out of there and do some tests."

Becky walked towards her car.

"No, Mrs Finnegan, your car's not going anywhere, and even if it could, you can't move it until they've finished taking some measurements. As I said, when we get the all clear, we'll go in my car."


Brandon and the other men waited outside the castle doors for Pat to come back with the Taser.

"At last! Did you get it?" Brandon asked.

"Yes, I brought four - one each," Pat responded.

"Four! The only reason I told you to bring *one* was in case we needed it, which is most unlikely. Well,

we're not going to find him standing here. Remember lads it's a big place with lots of places to hide. We'll start downstairs and make our way up, floor by floor, and make sure your radios are on," Brandon commanded.

"All clear!" came over the radio from Pat who had gone down into the kitchen.

"All clear in the library!" came from one of the others.

"Great Hall - all clear!"

"Clear in this back room."

"West side rooms all clear," came from Pat.

"I'm just checking the last room on the east side, then I'll meet you all back at the bottom of the grand stairs," Brandon said to them on his radio.

"Right, same method of search on the next floor," Brandon said.

They made their way along the corridor, checking each room.

"Nothing on this floor; he's got to be up there somewhere," Pat said looking up the other staircase.

"How many rooms in this place?" Kieran asked.

"Haven't a clue, but we're going to have to check them all," Brandon said. "Okay, ready, same as before."

Brandon was first to go up the stairs, when he heard, "Pat, you seen Connor?"

"No, I thought he was with you."

Brandon came back down the few steps he had gone up. "Where was he last?" he asked them.

"I saw him go in the last room up at the end there," Kieran said.

They all rushed down the corridor to the room and went in.

"He's not in here," Pat said, alarmed.

"Look he cannot just disappear without any trace or without any of us hearing anything," Brandon said, sounding concerned. "Come on lads, we're going to tear this place apart until we find him!" he said. "No more splitting up – we'll search together."    After systematically searching every room, they came to the last one.

"Where does that little door over there go to?" Kieran asked.

"Don't know; there's only one way to find out," Pat answered.

Kieran opened it, to see a narrow staircase.    "I think it goes up to the roof - he's got to be up there! Trouble is, we can only go up in single file. If he's waiting at the top, the first up wouldn't stand a chance."

"You've got your Taser haven't you?" Brandon said.

"What - me first?" Kieran said, alarmed.

"Well, you found the door.  If it makes you feel better, Pat will be behind you."

"Will I?"

"Look, we've got a job to do here.  Let's get on with it!" Brandon said to them.

Slowly Kieran crept up the winding stone steps, till he was faced with another small door.

After turning to make sure Pat was still behind him, he quickly opened the door and rushed out onto the roof, followed by Pat and Brandon.

They were confronted by the sight of the one-eyed man, standing on the edge of the parapet wall, holding Connor above his head.  Suddenly he flung

Connor at them, knocking Brandon and Kieran to the floor, with Connor on top of them.

"I, mighty Balor, will destroy you all!" he said, coming towards them.

Pat didn't hesitate to fire his Taser at him. Balor turned towards Pat, giving Brandon and Kieran time to get back on their feet. Balor ripped the Taser barbs from his body and grabbed hold of Pat, lifting him up above his head to throw him off the roof.

"Mother of God, fire your Tasers!" Pat screamed out.

They fired simultaneously, and the voltage made him drop Pat to the floor as he fell backwards against the parapet wall.

"Is he out?" Kieran asked.

"With that voltage I should think we've killed him!" Brandon said, walking over and kicking him with his boot. The groan told them otherwise.

"Quick, Kieran, give me a hand to cuff him," Brandon said.

"I think we'd better use mine as well. I don't think one pair will hold him."

After checking that Pat and Connor were all right, Brandon looked over the wall.

"It could have been worse; it's a long way down there - if he had chucked you over."

"I'll radio for the medics to come, meanwhile let's get him down."

"That's going to be fun - getting him down those winding stairs."

"If I had my way, Kieran, I'd throw him over the side; it would be quicker," Pat said.

"That's not what we're about, Pat!"

"I was joking, Brandon."

They carried him over to the top of the stairs and Kieran went down backwards with a foot in each hand, while Pat held him under the arms.

"He's so heavy! I'm having a job to lift him with my back bent over like this. Can't we drag him down?"

"You're right there, Pat! Yeah, let's drag him. He's out cold - I don't expect he'll feel anything; anyway, Brandon's not here to see."

"That was easier! Only two more flights to go," Pat said at the bottom of the tower steps.

At the bottom of the grand stairs, Brandon met them, "What're you two puffing for?"

"He weighs a ton!" Pat said.

"You can thank God it's not the Sarge you're carrying; *that's* a ton," Brandon chuckled. "Well you can dump him down there. I've radioed for the van; it'll be more secure than the car," Brandon said to them.

"Thank the saints for that! I couldn't have carried him any further," Pat said, letting go of the arms.

The thud to the ground made the man groan again, but this time he opened his eyes.

"Oh, my head! What's going on? What am I doing on the floor?"
They looked at him cautiously.

"So, Balor, you're not so mighty now, are you?" Brandon said to him.

"*Who*? My name's not Balor, it's Duffy. Why 'ave you got my hands tied behind me?"

"Mister, you're one weird man," Pat said to him.
The van pulled up outside.

"Good, I'll feel happier when this weirdo's in the van," Brandon said.

"I'm glad it's you in charge, Brandon, having to fill out the paperwork on this one," Pat said to him.

"Yeah, it's going to raise a few questions," he replied.

Standing outside, waiting to go in, were Tommy and Becky.

As they brought the captive out, Becky said, "Duffy!"

"Missus, I don't know what I've done wrong. Why are you having them take me away?"

"Get him in there as quick as you can, lads," Brandon said.

As they closed the door of the van, all that could be heard was, "Missus, help me! Don't let them take me away!"

Becky stood and watched the van disappear down the drive.

"I don't understand. Is *Duffy* responsible for all that's gone on here?" she asked Tommy.

"It looks like it."

"What will happen to him?"

"They'll put him in the cells overnight and then, judging by his state of mind, I should think he'll end up in one of those psychiatric places. I'm no psychiatrist, but I think he's suffering from schizophrenia."

"I still think he's possessed," Becky replied.

Tommy had already made his views on the subject clear. He said, "Look, I think it's time we had that tea, Mrs Finnegan. Shall we go in?"

"You sit down there and I'll put the kettle on," Tommy said.

"So, I was right about the room – that Sean was in there?" Becky asked, fearful of the answer.

"I know I said we'd have to wait, but yes it does look likely that it is him."

Becky burst into tears.

Knowing that she didn't have any family near, he said, "Would you like me to ring my wife, to pick you up and take you back to Maggie's?"

"Would you?" she responded, tearfully.

"I'll do it now. Hi, it's me; are you doing anything? Look, I'm up at the castle with Mrs Finnegan and she's just had some bad news. I was wondering if you could pick her up and take her back to Maggie's? I've got to wait here until the forensic guys have finished. Twenty minutes? Thanks, Doreen."


Fortunately for Connor he wasn't badly hurt and, after some attention from the medics, he was able to walk down with assistance.

"Glad to see you back with us, Connor," Brandon said, as he came out to where they had all gathered.

"I'm probably more pleased to see you guys. I thought I was a gonner when he grabbed me."

"How did you get past us and end up on that roof? As far as I could see, there was only one way up there and we were by the stairs," Pat asked.

"All I can remember is going in the room and, seeing that it was empty, I turned to come out. Then suddenly I was pulled backwards up against the panelled wall, and it opened. That was it, until I came to on the roof."

"Sounds as if there must be a secret passage from that room to the tower roof."

"The place is probably riddled with them, Pat, and as far as I'm concerned, they can stay there. We're all done here — let's go and have that celebration drink, lads."

"You buying then, Brandon?"

"Nope, you are Pat."

# Chapter 15

"Come and sit down, my dear," Maggie said as Doreen brought Becky into the room. "I gather they found him then?"

"Apparently, until he is formally identified, they can't say, but Officer Deneen told me it probably is him. And I know it *is* Sean, Maggie. What am I going to do now?"

"Well, my dear, we're just going to get through it; that's what we're going to do. Now you just sit there and I'll put the kettle on."

"It was Duffy all along, Maggie. He had been killing them!"

"*Duffy!* How do they know that? He hasn't got the brains to do such a thing," Maggie responded.

"They tell me he was hiding in the tunnel that led to the cellar room. When they found him he rushed out and I ran him down. Oh Maggie, it was awful!"

"What do mean, dear - you ran him down? How?"

"I had just come through the gates and he ran out of the trees. I didn't have time to stop. I thought I'd killed him. I don't think I'll ever get it out of my head."

"Are you saying he's *dead*?"

"No, after the ambulance came and they put him on the stretcher he woke up and ran off to the castle. It was weird: when he opened his eyes on that stretcher his face changed. He called himself 'King Balor'. The voice wasn't his - it was as if he was possessed."

"So is he still in the castle?"

"No, they got him, and took him away."

"I always said he wasn't right in the head! The first day I saw him standing there with his daddy in my kitchen, I knew there was something not right about him."

"I don't think I can ever go back there, Maggie. I wish we had never come to Ireland, then Sean would still be alive."

"You couldn't have known all this was going to happen, my dear."

"That's the thing, Maggie - we were warned to go back by an old tinker women on the road when we got here. She knew! She said that, unless we did, Sean's fate would be set in stone and my son would be next."

"My dear, these tinkers say all sorts of things to tourists. It's what they do to get money."
Doreen nodded.

"That's what Sean said, Maggie, but at that time I didn't have Finbar. I didn't even know I was pregnant!"

"Well dear, sometimes the Good Lord speaks to us in many ways and if he's sent a tinker to do it, then

who am I to say otherwise. I'll tell you one thing, my dear, Finbar's safe here (so are you) and you can stay as long as you like. Now drink up your tea."

Tommy made his way back down into the tunnel.

"How's it going, Aaron?" he asked.

"We are about to move him. I've been in many a place where there's a body, but never anywhere like this. I've got to confess, it gives you the creeps in here."

"I'll second that!" said one of the forensic team and another nodded.

While they were zipping up the body bag, Tommy walked over to a section of the cave wall and with his finger traced the outline of two fresh carvings in the rock.

"Anything of interest for us to look at?" Aaron asked.

"Might be. The last two times I was down here I noticed there were seven pairs of these eye shapes carved in the rock, now there's eight," Tommy said.

Aaron made his way over. "It looks as if the killer was keeping a count of eyes removed. He must be some sick weirdo! But then there's lots of them out there."

"Fortunately this type of stuff doesn't happen every day," Tommy replied.

"Right lads, are we ready to move him?" Aaron said. "You coming, Tommy?"

"You go on and I'll catch you up; I just want to study these shapes a bit longer."

Tommy had decided to take a photo of the carvings. As he stood there about to do so, the

temperature in the cave suddenly dropped and an overwhelming feeling that someone was behind him made him stop and slowly turn around. For a split second he saw the figure of a one-eyed man looking at him.

"Mary and the saints!" he gasped, as he ran for the exit.

"You all right, Tommy? You look as if you've seen a ghost," Aaron said.

He didn't say anything about what he thought he'd seen, as they wouldn't have believed him. Then, how could they, as he didn't believe it himself?

"Look, you all done here? I need to get to Murphy's and have a drink!"

"I would join you, but it looks as if it's going to be a late one for me," Aaron said.

"Evening, Tommy, you on or off duty?" Danny asked.

"Off, and after the day I've had, I need a little more than my usual!"

"Sounds like you had a rough time. Hey, you found that Duffy yet?"

"Yeah, we found him!"

"Was he in that ditch, as I thought?" he chuckled.

"Far from it, Danny."

"You're not giving much away; so where was he then?"

"I shouldn't be telling you, Danny, but as sure as Mrs Malone's got an old cow, you'll be hearing all about it. We've arrested Duffy for murder."

"*Duffy* a *murderer*? You got it all wrong; the only thing he could murder is his drink. No that's all wrong, Tommy. I can't believe it!"

"It's true - he was hiding in a tunnel with the body of that Sean Finnegan."

"What tunnel? Where?" Danny asked.

"Up at the castle. It was an old tunnel that led to a cave adjoining the castle; been there for centuries and no one knew it was there, except Duffy. In all the time you've known him, did he ever act strange, or talk with a weird voice?"

"We are talking about Duffy? He was always strange, and after a session of drink you had a job to understand him. Is that what you mean?"

"No, I think he's lost it, Danny. He thinks he's 'King Balor'; well that's what he called himself."

"Balor, you say - as in the Balor of folklore?" Danny laughed.

"That's the one. Anyway, they've carted him off."

"Old Duffy, a murderer! I would never have guessed. Hey, Michael! Did you hear? Old Duffy's been taken away for murder?" he called across the room.

"Get away with you! I don't believe it!"

"Well, I'd better get going home to Mrs Deneen. Thanks for the drink."

"If you hear anymore, Tommy . . ."

"Yeah, I know, Danny."


"Maggie, it's only me!" he called out.

"Hello, Tommy - in here!"

"I thought I'd see how Mrs Finnegan is. Is she around?"

"She's having a lie down. I gave her something to help her sleep, poor thing. Nasty shock that for her."

"It's never easy, Maggie. Do you think I could have that Professor Trant's number? I need some information about the castle."

"Well sure, I've got it here in my book somewhere," she said, turning the pages. "Ah! This is it. Something about the castle you say?"

"It's only something that Mrs Finnegan said today, to do with all that weird stuff about ghosts and people being possessed. I told her I didn't believe in it all; I just want to make sure what I think is right."

"So you think he might be able to help you on the subject?"

"He might be able to; those professor types are into that sort of stuff aren't they?"

"I don't really know. I know he's an expert on Irish history and folklore, but whether he knows about that stuff, you'll just have to ask him. Anyway, tell him you know me. I'm sure he will oblige; we go back a long way."

"I will do; thanks, Maggie. Well, I suppose I'd better get next door. I'll drop in tomorrow some time and see her."

"We'll be here, Tommy."


"Morning, my dear. How do you feel today?"

"What was that you gave me last night? I slept like a log."

"Only a herb; we've used it in my family for years - has none of those nasty side-effects that all this modern stuff has. So, my dear, what's planned for today?"

"I'm not sure, Maggie. I suppose I have to wait until Officer Deneen contacts me."

"He came in last night to see how you were. I told him you were asleep and he said he would call in and see you today. After all this is over, do you think you'll stay here?"

"To be honest, Maggie, I don't think I will. Apart from you, I don't really know anyone. No, I'll probably go back home."

"I don't blame you, my dear; too many bad memories I should think. What will you do with the castle?"

"Try and sell it . . . but who would want to buy it with three recent deaths and a ghost?"

"Oh, my dear, you don't really believe in ghosts do you? I thought it turned out to be Duffy?"

"I think he was possessed by an evil spirit that made him do it, Maggie."

"Well, my dear, whatever it was, he's safely locked away now, or will be."

"Maggie, I'll be going to church this Sunday. Will you be okay to look after Finbar?"

"Of course, my dear. Prayer is important at a time like this."


"Hello, Becky! We didn't think we'd see you, after hearing the bad news," Carley said, giving her a hug.

"I needed to come, Carley."

"Of course you did; you need people around you and that's what we're here for. Listen my offer still stands – if you need anything, or if you want me to visit you at the castle."

"Thanks, Carley, but I think I'll be going back to America as soon as the funeral is over."

"Is your husband being buried here?"

"I did think about taking him home, but all his family are buried at Father Dorian's church, so I thought it would be right for him to be buried with them."

"Oh okay, but wouldn't it be nice for you to have his grave to visit?" Carley said.

"If I had taken him back, I would have had him cremated anyway; at least this way he's with his family. Is that nice pastor around? I need to talk to him."

"Sean, yes he's here somewhere, probably in the prayer room. Best time to get him is after the service but you have to be quick - there's always someone wanting to speak to him. I tell you what, I'll make sure I grab him before anyone else for you."

"Thanks, Carley. I know that if I had stayed, we would have become good friends."

"Thank you, Becky. I know we would have done, but you haven't gone yet," she said, finding two seats.

The worship group started playing their beautiful songs and again Becky found them really moving. She looked around and could see that people truly meant what they were singing. They were worshiping God with all their hearts, not just singing along routinely.

Pastor Sean welcomed everyone and began his message. This time Becky listened attentively. Throughout her childhood she'd attended church but she'd never heard anything like this. It was as though someone had switched on a light in a room she hadn't realised was so dark.

"Hello Becky; so sorry to hear the bad news about your husband. Is there anything I can do, or help with?"

"Thank you, Pastor, but it's all been arranged."

"Carley said you wanted to talk?"

"Yes, I do but do you mind if I ask you some questions first?"

"Please do!"

"Pastor, do you believe people can be possessed by an evil spirit?"

"Yes I do. There's an example in the Bible where Jesus cast many demons from a man who was living naked among tombs and cutting himself."

"But what about modern times?"

"Yes, I can assure you it still happens. May I ask if there's a reason you're asking?"

"Let's just say you've confirmed something I was curious about. Is there anything that will overcome evil – like holy water or garlic or something?"

"There's a lot of superstition in things like that. But there is power in the name of Jesus and in God's word, the Bible. Having said that, I hope you're not even considering confronting anything evil on your own. Don't go near it. Now, is that it – or did you have any other questions?"

"Well, yes. About your preaching this morning: I always thought that you had to be a good person to go to Heaven, and I was so shocked to hear you say that's not the case."

"That's right, Becky. If it *was* none of us would make it, because we've all done wrong. That's why Jesus died. Take me, for example, I was once a drug addict living on the streets and stealing to feed my habit. I accepted Jesus when I was in prison."

"*Really?* I still don't understand though . . ."

"Well, imagine you're in court and you've been found guilty of a driving offence for which the fine is £1,000 or you go to prison. You don't have any money and you can't possibly pay. Then, to your surprise, the judge says: 'My son loves you so much that he will pay – if you accept the offer.'"

"Are you saying that we all go to Heaven, no matter what we've done?"

"No, I'm not. Even though it's a free gift, most people don't accept it."

"But *how* do you accept this gift?"

"You just tell him you want to. Speak to him. The Bible says: '*If you confess with your mouth the Lord Jesus and believe in your heart that God has raised him from the dead, you will be saved.*"

"Do I have to do that in church?"

"No, you can just speak to him when you're on your own if you prefer. Would you like to pray now?"

"I think I'll do it when I'm on my own, Pastor."

"Okay, Becky – it's your call. I'd like to give you this Bible – I think you'll find it helpful. Will we be seeing you next Sunday?"

"No, if all goes well I'll be on the plane going home."

"Well, I will pray for you; have a safe journey."


"Good service, my dear?"

"Yes, very good, Maggie. Any trouble with him?"

"No, he's a little angel; I'll miss him when he goes," Maggie said, tickling his tummy.

"Maggie, there's something I have to do at the castle tomorrow; can I ask you to mind him again."

"Are you sure you should be going there on your own? Why don't we come with you?"

"No Maggie, I don't want Finbar anywhere near there, now or in the future."

"My dear, it sounds serious; you're getting me worried."

"I know what I'm doing, Maggie. Besides, I have no choice. Can I ask you one more thing? If anything happens to me tomorrow and I don't return, can you make sure that my parents come and get Finbar?"

"Now you *are* worrying me! What is it you're going to do?"

"Have you heard the saying, 'Face your demon'? Well, that's what I have to do. Look, Maggie, I have to ask you again; tell me you will make sure Finbar's okay?"

"Of course I will, dear."

Satisfied that Maggie would keep her promise, Becky spent the afternoon absorbed in reading the Bible, while Finbar slept peacefully.


"Constable Deneen, please come in," the professor said, showing him to the front room. "Please sit down. So, you have questions about the castle?"

"Yes, or rather more about your opinion on what's gone on up there. You know there have been some deaths there recently?"

"Yes, two of the Finnegans."

"Well, there's been another."

"Not that young Becky's husband? She said she had a feeling he was there all along, in the room beneath the castle. In fact, to be precise, it's a cave."

"You know all about that?"

"Yes, we discovered (from the book) there was another entrance to the cave, up by the big stone. The stones at the entrance were too big and heavy for us to move, so we had to leave it."

"Look, what I've come to talk about is: what element of truth is there in this story of Balor?"

"Balor! His name keeps coming up. If you had asked me two weeks ago, I would have said he's just a myth. But since having his book in my possession, I'm not so sure."

"What, are you saying he could be alive?"

"Not physically; more his spirit. You see, he was a Druid and they practised all sorts of dark evil. It was powerful stuff that they believed in and, because of that, it has been known for such an evil to linger in time."

"I'm not saying I believe in all this stuff, but could his spirit possess someone, enough to make them kill?"

"I would say 'yes' and, in the case of Balor, from what I've found in the book, he was as evil as they came."

"So why would he have had it in for the Finnegan family?"

"I think it's to do with the castle and its name. Apparently, before the castle was there, it was a place where the Druids worshiped, and sacrificed people in the cave. The big stone was put there as a monument to Balor, and to strike fear into the people, even from miles away. Did you notice the eye shape carved into it? The book says that beneath it is his evil eye, which keeps his spirit alive."

"No, I can't say I did, but there's plenty of them carved in the wall of the cave."

"So you found it then? And you say there are *lots* of them?"

"Yes, interestingly there appears to be two carved in it when someone is killed there."

"That ties up with the sacrifices. Every time they performed one, they would remove the victim's eyes and offer them to Balor. I can understand the stone connection, but I've been asking myself: what is the connection between *the castle* and Balor? Then I found it in the book. When the castle was built nearby, its original name was: 'Caislén a t'Súil Olc (Castle of the Evil Eye) but as time went on they dropped the 'Evil' out of it. I think the reason he unleashed his anger on the Finnegans was for changing the name to Finnegan Castle."

"Like Balor's revenge?" Constable Deneen asked.

"Precisely. Balor's revenge. Constable Deneen, would you say there's any chance of me taking a look in that cave?"

"When we've finished with the case, that would be up to Mrs Finnegan, but if you'll take my advice, I wouldn't venture in there on your own."

"I thought you said you didn't believe in anything like that."

"I don't. I mean: you could get hurt down there and nobody would know."

"Of course, Constable Deneen," the professor said, smiling.

"Did you say you have Balor's book?"

"Yes, why?"

"You'd better look after it. I'm not saying it will, but it might be needed to answer some questions."

"Well, if you need me to explain anything, I'll be pleased to help."

"As I said, it probably won't come to that. On the face of it, it looks like a case of a killing by an insane person. Well, thanks for your time."

As the professor showed him out, he said, "So, you still think the Balor legend is too far-fetched?"

"Shall we say, Professor, it's an open subject and a story I shall remember for a very long time."


Becky needed all the courage she could muster to face what she was about to do and, knowing Maggie would try one more time to stop her, she decided to get up before Maggie awoke. Kissing Finbar on the forehead, she left for the castle.

Arriving outside, she made her way over to Duffy's shed and let herself in. Looking around, she found what she was hoping for, a can of lawnmower fuel. With it, she walked towards the big doors of the castle, unlocked them then went in, and down to the kitchen. The first thing she saw was that the big dresser had been pushed away from the wall, revealing a pile of brick rubble and the door.

As fear began to engulf her, Becky took from her pocket the bookmark Pastor Sean had given her. She began to read out some of the phrases from Psalm 91 for protection: '*You will not fear the terror of night . . . no harm will befall you . . . He will command his angels to guard you . . .*'.

She gave the door a gentle push. As it swung open, she felt the chilled, stagnant air rush up to her. She groped for the light switch.

"Balor! You foul demon! You might have taken my husband, but you will not have my child! This far and

no further - do you hear me? I bind you in Jesus' name; go back to the depths from where you came!"

The light flickered off. Then from out of the darkness came deep laughter followed by, "Who are you to command me with your meaningless words? Jesus - I know, but you and your words are weak and without power. I am Balor, King of the Fomorians, King of the Druids. I take whom I choose; I possess whom I want to; the child is mine!"

"You will never have him, you foul demon! He will never live here!" Becky answered angrily.

The light in the room started to flicker violently, turning to a greenish hue, and before Becky's eyes, Balor appeared at the bottom of the stairs and started to make his way towards her.

"The child's fate has been set. He will come in his lifetime. I will have my revenge on the Finnegan name," Balor bellowed, as he made his way up towards her.

She unscrewed the lid of the fuel can and threw it down the stairs at him. With the words: "Burn in hell!" she tossed a match down the stairs. A fireball engulfed the room and roared up the stairs towards her. Becky just managed to move to one side of the door as the ball of flames engulfed the back of the dresser. Thick smoke soon started to fill the room as the fire had now spread from the dresser to the kitchen. Then from out of the doorway stepped Balor, his clothes and hair on fire. Becky slowly backed away from the doorway towards the kitchen door, choking from the smoke. She could see the face of Balor grinning at her, as if he was enjoying the flames. She knew she had only a short distance to go to the door, then she could run up the stairs and out

of the castle. As if he knew what she was thinking, the kitchen door slammed shut behind her. She rushed forwards and reached for the door handle, desperately trying to open it, and looking behind her as she did. She could see that Balor was just a few steps from her and that any second he would have her.

From the depths of her spirit, she shouted "*Jesus!*"

Balor knew the name was said with a power that he had to obey. The door slowly opened. Becky didn't question what had just happened; she rushed up the stairs, climbed into her car and sped up the drive. Outside the iron gates she stopped and looked back to see the castle engulfed in flames.

# Chapter 16

One of the Americans could see that the glasses were getting empty and said to Duffy, "Hold the story while I'll get us all some more drinks."

His friend gave him a hand, leaving the two women with Duffy.

While waiting for the drinks to arrive, Duffy reached into his pocket and took out an apple, then produced a large penknife and sliced off a piece.

"Would you cailins like a bit of my apple?" he said to the women.

"No, thank you," they replied, not relishing the thought of eating something that his rusty old knife had cut into (and who knows what else).

Duffy leaned over to one of them and, with a big grin, said: "You've got a lovely pair of eyes, cailin."

The woman turned to her friend and said, "Did he just make a pass at me?"

The thought of it made the pair giggle.

"Evening, Tommy."

"Evening Danny; has he been behaving himself?" Tommy replied, nodding towards Duffy.

"Yeah, he's been telling us all a story of the Finnegan's castle."

"I would keep an eye on him, Danny."

"He's all right, Tommy. You've been a Garda too long," he replied.

"I'm just saying - the memories of it might start something off in him."

"Like what?"

"Look, I think I'd better stay around until you close," Tommy responded.


"Same again bar tender. Hey that's some old character you've got over there," the American said to Danny.

"Old Duffy? For sure he is. In fact, he's quite famous," Danny replied.

"Famous! For what?"

"Murder," Tommy said. "He's not long been let out of a high security prison for the mentally ill. He served thirty years for the gruesome killing of three people, and the only reason they let him out is because they think, because of his age, he will be no threat to anyone."

"How old is he then?" the American asked.

"He's ninety, and with poor health, he hasn't got long for this world; God bless his soul. But, you know, all the time he was in there he said he didn't do it. No one ever believed his story of a one-eyed man that did it. Strange thing though, they never found the weapon, or their eyes."

"It's true - he was hiding in a tunnel with the body of that Sean Finnegan."

"What tunnel? Where?" Danny asked.

"Up at the castle. It was an old tunnel that led to a cave adjoining the castle; been there for centuries and no one knew it was there, except Duffy. In all the time you've known him, did he ever act strange, or talk with a weird voice?"

"We are talking about Duffy? He was always strange, and after a session of drink you had a job to understand him. Is that what you mean?"

"No, I think he's lost it, Danny. He thinks he's 'King Balor'; well that's what he called himself."

"Balor, you say - as in the Balor of folklore?" Danny laughed.

"That's the one. Anyway, they've carted him off."

"Old Duffy, a murderer! I would never have guessed. Hey, Michael! Did you hear? Old Duffy's been taken away for murder?" he called across the room.

"Get away with you! I don't believe it!"

"Well, I'd better get going home to Mrs Deneen. Thanks for the drink."

"If you hear anymore, Tommy . . ."

"Yeah, I know, Danny."


"Maggie, it's only me!" he called out.

"Hello, Tommy - in here!"

"I thought I'd see how Mrs Finnegan is. Is she around?"

"She's having a lie down. I gave her something to help her sleep, poor thing. Nasty shock that for her."

"It's never easy, Maggie. Do you think I could have that Professor Trant's number? I need some information about the castle."

"Well sure, I've got it here in my book somewhere," she said, turning the pages. "Ah! This is it. Something about the castle you say?"

"It's only something that Mrs Finnegan said today, to do with all that weird stuff about ghosts and people being possessed. I told her I didn't believe in it all; I just want to make sure what I think is right."

"So you think he might be able to help you on the subject?"

"He might be able to; those professor types are into that sort of stuff aren't they?"

"I don't really know. I know he's an expert on Irish history and folklore, but whether he knows about that stuff, you'll just have to ask him. Anyway, tell him you know me. I'm sure he will oblige; we go back a long way."

"I will do; thanks, Maggie. Well, I suppose I'd better get next door. I'll drop in tomorrow some time and see her."

"We'll be here, Tommy."


"Morning, my dear. How do you feel today?"

"What was that you gave me last night? I slept like a log."

"Only a herb; we've used it in my family for years - has none of those nasty side-effects that all this modern stuff has. So, my dear, what's planned for today?"

"I'm not sure, Maggie. I suppose I have to wait until Officer Deneen contacts me."

"So the yarn he's been telling us is true?" the American said.

"Most of it is, but I don't know about the leprechaun bit. Who knows with old Duffy? He's always been a great storyteller, with a big imagination. The doctors found out that it goes back to his childhood. Apparently his daddy was always filling his head with old stories of Balor, the one-eyed Druid. I reckon he heard it so many times that he thinks Balor is real. It's left him on the brink of insanity," Tommy said.

"So he did do it?" the American said.

"Truth? I'm still not quite sure; a fool yes, but a psychopathic killer?" Danny questioned.

Tommy didn't say anything.

"Another thing, why didn't Becky just leave the place? It seems a bit drastic to burn it down," the American asked.

"Rumour has it, she did it in case her son, being the last of the male Finnegans, returned when he was older," Tommy told him.

"So did the castle ever get rebuilt?"

"It's strange you should ask. Only last week I heard there's builders started on site," Danny replied.

"Do you think it's the Finnegan son rebuilding it after all this time?"

"Who knows? But if it is, and what we have just heard is true, Mother of God help him," Danny said, making the sign of the cross on his chest.

Their conversation was stopped short by the words: "I think he's dead!" which came from one of the women at the table.

Everyone looked across to see Duffy slumped over the table. Tommy rushed over, followed by Danny.

Tommy leaned over to check for a pulse, and as he did, Duffy slowly rose from the table, revealing a face that was not his. Tommy stood there in horror to see that it was a face he seen once before. It was the face of Balor.

The women screamed as he reached out and grabbed one of them. The grinning face was the last thing her eyes would ever see.

"Mother of God, Balor is back!" were the last words of Tommy, while all who were in the bar were screaming and trying to get away.

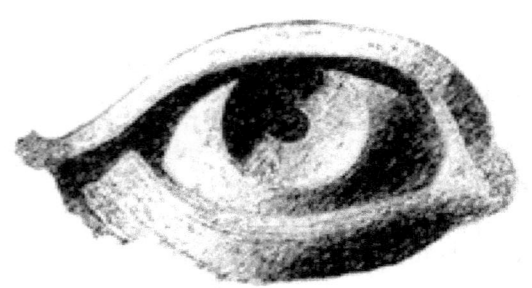